That one kiss didn't mean anything

Not to him, not to her, either, Max rationalized. Sarah wasn't the type for a flirtation or a brief affair. She didn't date, and if she did, she would take it seriously. Max knew that.

But just a glance in her direction, seeing her hair tossed by the breeze, dark wisps on her cheek, watching her bite into a ripe strawberry, her lips stained red, he was not ready to say goodbye to her for good.

Max drank from the wine bottle and tasted her lips there. It wasn't enough. He wanted more than a taste. He needed more. Maybe it was the sun. Maybe it was the warm air. Maybe it was her. He leaned across the blanket and framed her face in his hands. Sarah's eyes widened. Such huge blue eyes.

What was so wrong with a kiss—or two—between friends?

Dear Reader,

As the days get shorter and the approaching holidays bring a buzz to the crisp air, nothing quite equals the joy of reuniting with family and catching up on the year's events. This month's selections all deal with family matters, be it making one's own family, dealing with family members or doing one's family duty.

Desperate to save his family ranch, the hero in Elizabeth Harbison's *Taming of the Two* (#1790) enters into a bargain that could turn a pretend relationship into the real deal. This is the second title in the SHAKESPEARE IN LOVE trilogy. A die-hard bachelor gets a taste of what being a family man is like when he rescues a beautiful stranger and her adorable infant from a deadly blizzard, in Susan Meier's *Snowbound Baby* (#1791)—part of the author's BRYANT BABY BONANZA continuity. Carol Grace continues her FAIRY TALE BRIDES miniseries with *His Sleeping Beauty* (#1792) in which a woman sheltered by her overprotective parents gains the confidence to strike out on her own after her handsome—but cynical—neighbor catches her sleepwalking in his garden! Finally, in *The Marine and Me* (#1793), the next installment in Cathie Linz's MEN OF HONOR series, a soldier determined to outwit his matchmaking grandmother and avoid the marriage landmine gets bushwhacked by his supposedly dowdy neighbor.

Be sure to come back next month when Karen Rose Smith and Shirley Jump put their own spins on Shakespeare and the Dating Game, respectively!

Happy reading.

Ann Leslie Tuttle
Associate Senior Editor

Please address questions and book requests to:
Silhouette Reader Service
U.S.: 3010 Walden Ave., P.O. Box 1325, Buffalo, NY 14269
Canadian: P.O. Box 609, Fort Erie, Ont. L2A 5X3

CAROL GRACE

His Sleeping Beauty

Fairy Tale Brides

SILHOUETTE *Romance*®

Published by Silhouette Books

America's Publisher of Contemporary Romance

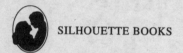 SILHOUETTE BOOKS

ISBN 0-373-19792-6

HIS SLEEPING BEAUTY

Books by Carol Grace

Silhouette Romance

Make Room for Nanny #690
A Taste of Heaven #751
Home Is Where the Heart Is #882
Mail-Order Male #955
The Lady Wore Spurs #1010
*Lonely Millionaire #1057
*Almost a Husband #1105
*Almost Married #1142
*The Rancher and the Lost
  Bride* #1153
†Granted: Big Sky Groom #1277
†Granted: Wild West Bride #1303
*†Granted: A Family for
  Baby* #1345
Married to the Sheik #1391
The Librarian's Secret Wish #1473
Fit for a Sheik #1500
Taming the Sheik #1554
A Princess in Waiting #1588

Falling for the Sheik #1607
Pregnant by the Boss! #1666
***Beauty and the Big Bad
  Wolf* #1767
**Cinderellie! #1775
**His Sleeping Beauty #1792

Silhouette Desire

Wife for a Night #1118
*The Heiress Inherits a
  Cowboy* #1145
Expecting… #1205
The Magnificent M.D. #1284

*Miramar Inn
†Best-Kept Wishes
**Fairy-Tale Brides

CAROL GRACE

has always been interested in travel and living abroad. She spent her junior year of college in France and toured the world working on the hospital ship *HOPE*. She and her husband spent the first year and a half of their marriage in Iran, where they both taught English. She has studied Arabic and Persian languages. Then, with their toddler daughter, they lived in Algeria for two years.

Carol says that writing is another way of making her life exciting. Her office is her mountaintop home, which overlooks the Pacific Ocean and which she shares with her inventor husband, their daughter, who just graduated college, and their teenage son.

Prologue

Standing on his flagstone patio some time after midnight, Max Monroe almost missed seeing the mysterious figure dressed in white at his back fence. He stubbed out his cigar and took a few steps forward. There she was under the trees. Then she was gone. He shook his head. Real, or an illusion? He'd had wine with dinner, but not enough to bring on hallucinations. The hair on the back of his neck stood up and he felt a cool breeze on his arms. Who was it? What was it?

It certainly wasn't his neighbor Mary, a petite, silver-haired, lively older lady who lived next door was away on a Caribbean cruise. He'd been told that her niece was going to be house-sitting and by the way, if he wouldn't mind looking in on her once or twice, Mary would be very grateful.

He owed it to Mary. She'd been more than helpful when he was moving in, letting the phone men into his house to set up his Internet connection, recommending gardeners and a cleaning crew.

According to Mary, her niece, Sarah, was too quiet, too shy and too studious. She was liable to stay indoors too much and keep to herself. Sarah needed a nudge to get out and smell the roses, which by the way, grew in abundance behind Mary's house. Not the type of woman he'd be interested in getting to know, but still, what could he say?

Eager to make friends in the neighborhood and to repay his neighbor for her generosity, Max promised to look in on Sarah, though he doubted he could lure her out of her shell, if she was really as shy as her aunt said. When he'd seen a strange VW Bug in the driveway this afternoon, he'd phoned the house and knocked on her door, but no one answered. She had to be there so why didn't she come to the door? Nobody's that shy. But, what the hell, he'd tried, and he'd done his job.

Max took a sip of coffee from his mug while he watched and waited for the vision to appear again. If it really was a person. If he'd really seen anything at all. In the meantime, he surveyed his landscaped yard illuminated by the silvery moonlight, and his rock-rimmed lighted pool with pride of ownership. His new home was more than a house. It was a symbol that he'd arrived. The poverty of his childhood, the apartments he'd lived in, one after another, were finally all in the past. This place was his, all his. The next day he was having his first party there.

Aha, there it was again, the flutter of white shimmering in the moonlight. This time he was going to get to the bottom of this mystery and find out who it was. He set his coffee cup down and strode across the damp lawn until he stopped suddenly and stared.

There under the fragrant eucalyptus trees was a woman in a white gown only ten feet away from him. Her dark hair was tousled by the breeze, her sheer gown billowed, giving her an ethereal look. Under the gown he could make out the outline of her breasts and hips. His body reacted as if he'd been given a shot of adrenaline and he felt a sharp quickening of his senses. Not that he was gawking, but he was human, wasn't he?

She was slender, this vision, but had curves in all the right places. He tilted his head and watched as she moved a little closer. Who was this ghostly creature? As he stood there, she bent over and picked up a handful of eucalyptus nuts.

"Hello?" he said.

She murmured something and looked past him as if he wasn't there. It couldn't be Mary's niece, the woman who had to be coaxed outside, could it? Maybe she was sleepwalking and didn't know she was outside. Thank God he'd put a fence around the pool.

He'd seen a picture of her and this woman looked nothing like Mary's neice. In the photograph a serious bespectacled woman in cap and gown posed with fellow graduates on a college campus. This lovely creature was the complete opposite—so mysterious and romantic that he couldn't keep his eyes off of her.

He took her arm. She frowned and shook it off. He wasn't discouraged. He put his arm firmly around her shoulder and gently turned her toward her house. She continued to clutch the nuts in her hand, but she didn't resist. He murmured what he hoped were soothing words, but she didn't appear to be listening.

So he guided her into the house and up the stairs, clumsily bumping against the polished railing on one side and her hip on the other. The first bedroom door was open and a bed was so rumpled, it looked as if it had been slept in by someone who'd been tossing and turning.

"Is this it?" he said more to himself than to her. She didn't answer. He didn't expect her to, but she headed straight for the bed, as if on autopilot, put the eucalyptus nuts on the bedside table, then lay down, put her head on the pillow and closed her eyes.

He stood there for a long moment wondering what to do. Did sleepwalkers walk more than once a night? If so, should he lock her in or post himself at the door downstairs? He stared down at her pale, heart-shaped face, at the dark hair that was spread out on the pillow and felt totally bewildered. It didn't make sense. How could the shy, introverted woman he'd heard about have turned into an enchantress? He should really leave. Go out and lock the door behind him and check on her to-morrow.

Instead he just stood there, wondering if, like Sleeping Beauty, it would take a kiss to wake her. If it did, and she was startled, she might jump up and whack him over the head with that vase of flowers on the dresser. What did he have to lose? A lump on the head. An embarrassing explanation. He'd always been a risk-taker. So he leaned over and brushed his lips against hers. Soft, full lips. Tempting lips.

Instead of claiming another kiss, which was what he wanted to do, he decided not to press his luck and reluctantly drew back. She didn't wake up. She didn't leap up and smack him. She smiled. That was it. Just a smile. But what a sleepy, sexy smile it was.

Was she dreaming? Or was he? Did she know what had happened? Would she remember this tomorrow? Should he inform her? Was he crazy? He pulled a blanket up to her shoulders and ran his fingers over her bare shoulder where her nightgown had slipped down.

Tomorrow he'd have to alert Sleeping Beauty that, in case she didn't know it, she had a problem. Or rather, if she kept coming to his place in the middle of the night, *they* had a problem.

He had *no* intention of getting involved with a woman, any woman, no matter how beautiful or romantic. Especially if she really was Mary's niece. He could foresee acres of complications around the corner. But there could be nothing wrong with making a neighborly call on her. In fact, that's what he'd intended to do all along. It's what Mary had asked him to do.

But as he walked quietly down the carpeted stairs, he knew he wasn't fooling anyone. There was something about the woman that intrigued him. That made him want to find out what made her tick. Or to be more precise, what made her walk into his yard at night and collect eucalyptus nuts while sound asleep. It could be just her looks that attracted him, but he'd met dozens of beautiful women and had carefully kept them at arm's length—at least emotionally—which was where they belonged. He usually didn't pursue women, figuring they weren't worth the time and effort. And when they pursued him, he'd eventually ended things. Which was exactly what he'd probably do with this one, if…if it came to that. Which it wouldn't, because in the morning the mystery would be over. Tonight she'd stepped out of a dream and into his backyard. But tomorrow, he'd find out she was an ordinary woman and that would be the end of it. Wouldn't it?

Chapter One

At eight o'clock the next morning a loud roaring sound woke Sarah with a start. She sat bolt upright in bed and blinked. She'd been dreaming. She was wandering through a forest in the moonlight, dressed in a long white gown, lost and alone until she saw a dark, mysterious man through the trees. He took her arm and they strolled farther into the trees until…he kissed her. A most amazing kiss that made her tingle all over. That made her want to kiss him back. But before she could, he was gone and it was too late. He'd disappeared, leaving behind only the memory of his shadowy face and the way he tasted, of wine and cigar smoke and coffee.

She was surprised she was able to taste and smell in a dream. That was a first. Also a first to wake up and find her heart pounding and shivers running up and down her spine. Not only that, she'd awakened with her lips still tingling, but with a feeling of disappointment, disorientation and unfulfillment. Where was she? Who was he? What was wrong with her?

One good thing. She hadn't had an asthma attack in the middle of the night. She hadn't had one for a long time, but the memories of gasping for breath, staggering into a steam-filled bathroom and the ever-present inhaler she kept at hand even now, just in case, would always be there.

The sun was shining on unfamiliar, faux-finished, pale yellow walls. The air coming through the open window was perfumed with roses—instead of the traffic fumes she was used to. Considering her black thumb, the roses couldn't possibly be hers. The antique armoire in the corner was smoothly finished in an aged patina and not hers, either.

Then it all came back to her. Instead of sleeping in her own bed in her tiny apartment in crowded, foggy San Francisco, she was house-sitting at Aunt Mary's sprawling home some thirty miles south in Portola Valley, a suburb of the City by the Bay. And that buzzing sound? That was the man next door cutting down Aunt Mary's three-hundred-year-old oak tree! She'd been warned he might take advantage of her aunt's absence and attack the tree just because it was shading his swimming pool. Not on her watch he wouldn't. That was her primary job while she was there, to protect and preserve one defenseless tree.

She bounded out of bed, tore off her white cotton nightgown and tugged on a pair of drawstring pants, a comfortable faded T-shirt, and her large glasses, and ran on the filed floor through the house and out the back door.

"Just what do you think you're doing?" she shouted across the fence. She was wasting her breath. He didn't see her. He didn't hear her. But she saw him, all six-foot-something of muscular man, naked to the waist of his low-slung jeans.

She blinked. And stared. It was him. The man in her dreams. Then she shook her head. No, it couldn't be, because the man in her dreams lived in a forest, loved trees and would never hurt one. He didn't hear her, this tree killer, but she heard *him*, the whole neighborhood heard him.

Finally he turned off the chain saw, wiped the sweat from his forehead and looked over the fence.

"Hello," he said with a dazzling smile on his tanned face that she supposed charmed every woman he encountered. And made them forget he was doing something he shouldn't. But not her aunt. Not her, either, unless he put that chain saw down and swore never to use it again. "Did I wake you?"

"Me and the rest of Portola Valley. Yes, you did."

He didn't seem to get the message. Instead he merely set the saw on the ground and let his gaze roam over her baggy clothes. "Sleep well?" he asked as if this was an important question. He was anxious to hear her answer.

What did he care if she'd slept well, unless this was a chain-saw related question. Still, it was an odd question to ask a stranger. What did that have to do with anything? She decided he was just trying to change the subject. "What do you think you're doing?" she demanded. As if she didn't know.

"Just trimming the tree," he said, bracing his arms on the fence between the two properties. "Before it trims me. It's got some dead limbs I wouldn't want to fall on my house or yours for that matter. I'm new here." He reached over the fence to shake her hand. "I don't think we've met. Or have we?" He was staring at her intently as if he wasn't sure. But she was. They had not met anywhere, any time. Except maybe in her dream. If it had been in real life, she would have remembered. She didn't meet that many good-looking men. And when she did, she was tongue-tied and shy. Not today. Today she had something to say.

"No, I'm sure we haven't."

"Max Monroe," he said.

Gingerly she extended her hand and shook his, her small hand immediately engulfed in his, while trying not to stare at the rivulets of sweat that dripped across the well-defined muscles on his chest. What did the man do to keep in such good shape? Was he a professional athlete? Or did he go to a gym and work out with a personal trainer? Things she might have done if she weren't afraid of having an attack triggered by exercise. Never mind. She did what she could to keep in shape by walking to work in the city.

She couldn't remember what Aunt Mary had told her about him. She really hadn't been listening. Now she wished she had so she could pigeonhole him, and put him in a category the way she, as a social scientist, would do with a piece of historical information.

"You must be Mary's niece. She told me about you," he said. There she was at a disadvantage. He knew all about her, she knew nothing about him. Sarah wondered what her aunt had told him. That she was a nerd? That she didn't date and had no social life to speak of? That she worked too hard and needed a break along with some new clothes and a new attitude? Was that why he was looking at her as if he was trying to figure her out, as if she might be a creature from another world.

"Did she also tell you that's her tree you're hacking at?" Sarah asked.

"It's *our* tree," he said pleasantly, slapping the bark with one hand. "And I offered to keep it trimmed so it doesn't endanger either of our houses."

"That's good of you, but my aunt is more worried about the tree than her house. You can replace a house, but a tree like that…" She looked up into the branches that towered above her, and felt a little dizzy. That's what came from sleeping in a strange bed and being awakened so rudely and so suddenly. She'd been working long hours, too, trying to finish a project. Because of her past medical problems, she always tried to avoid the stress of deadlines by getting her work done ahead of time. Her aunt had said she looked pale and hoped she'd get some rest while she was house-sitting. Not with this Paul Bunyon next door, she wouldn't.

Sarah had been bogged down researching a paper about the gold rush for the next meeting of the Northern California Historical Society. She loved the subject, but with the hint of spring in the air and the promise of warm weather just around the corner, she'd been distracted.

Maybe she'd be able to concentrate better away from the office. She hoped so, because she'd informed the staff she'd be working from her aunt Mary's this week. Her boss wasn't too happy about it. In fact, Trudy had been in a bad mood for the past six months, uncharacteristically taciturn and closed off from the easy camaraderie they'd shared in the past. Still she agreed to Sarah's working from home for a week. After all, Sarah hadn't taken a vacation in three years.

She didn't need time off, no matter what other people thought. She might be a little dizzy right now, but it was only because she'd changed her environment. She'd gone from city to suburb, from concrete to grass and from tall buildings to tall trees. Speaking of trees, she really had to be firm with this man.

Sarah put her hand on the fence to steady herself and her arm brushed against his. She felt a zing of electricity run up her arm, but from the look on his handsome face, Max didn't feel anything at all. She really had to get a grip on her reactions. She jerked her arm away and took a deep breath.

"Just to give you some background, the tree is older than any building standing around here," she said, gathering her thoughts at last. "The tree was standing when the Ohlone Indians lived here. Why, they might have danced around it to celebrate the beginning of spring. They'd have their skin painted, and their long hair bound and dyed." She stared off into space, easily imagining the scene, almost hearing the beat of the drums. Her enthusiasm made her one of the foremost experts in her field; she lived and breathed the history of early California. If that made her a nerd, so be it.

"Really?" he said, raising an eyebrow, a half smile on his lips. "Funny you should mention it, because that's just what's going to happen here this afternoon."

"A Native American ceremony, here?" she asked, wide-eyed. Now that would be something to see.

"I don't know about the Indians, but there will be dancing, and you might see some dyed hair and some painted skin. You'll come by, won't you?"

"Come by?" she repeated. What on earth was he talking about? Why would she want to come by unless it was for real?

"To the pool party I'm throwing this afternoon. This house happens to be a great place for parties. Part of my job is entertaining clients and courting new ones. I've been afraid the noise of a party would disturb your aunt, so knowing she was going on vacation, I planned it for today. Now that you're here, I don't need to worry. See you at four."

"Uh…I'm not sure. I usually work on the weekends," she explained. No way was she going to a party to hang around a pool with a bunch of half-naked strangers. She hadn't come to the quiet of the suburbs to be forced into awkward and stressful social situations. She learned long ago to avoid anxiety-producing situations whenever possible. Let people think she was antisocial. Her life was just the way she wanted it. Besides, she had much too much work to do.

"Work, on a day like this?" he asked, with a glance at the blue sky above. "Three hundred years ago you wouldn't catch the Ohlone Indians working if they had a chance to play, would you?"

"Probably not," she admitted. "They took every opportunity to dance and sing and feast, but I'm not a Native American."

"But you know a lot about them," he said, scratching his chin thoughtfully.

"I should. It's my job to know about California's history." It's my life also, she thought. She never understood why anyone, Aunt Mary included, thought it wasn't enough of a life. Living in the past, some people said about her, shaking their heads. So what was wrong with that? The past was full of exotic characters, ranchers and explorers, swindlers and miners, spellbinders and promoters. In Sarah's experience, people today weren't all that exciting.

"So I heard," he said, leaning over the fence and studying her with narrowed gray eyes. She couldn't help thinking how unusual that was. She'd never known anyone with gray eyes. Gray eyes, a firm jaw and broad bronzed shoulders. What a combination. She suddenly felt breathless again. She inhaled deeply. She was fine. No wheezing, no reduced air flow. Just a case of jitters. Pretty silly for a twenty-five-year-old historical scholar. She'd better pull herself together and remember why she was there.

"About the tree," she said, shifting from one foot to the other. After all, that's what this was all about—the tree.

"Beautiful tree. Don't worry, I'd never do anything to endanger it. Especially now that I know what it's been through in the past three hundred years. You'll have to see it from this side."

"Oh, I don't think that's necessary, the view from here is enough. I appreciate it just fine so don't count on me, I mean…"

"Come on over anytime," he said, as if she hadn't explained she wasn't coming at all. "The band will be tuning up around four."

"A pool party would be wasted on me," she said. "I don't swim."

"Don't or can't?" he asked, drawing his eyebrows together in a puzzled look.

"Both. Either." There. That ought to get him off her case. She didn't have to explain why she didn't swim, run, jog or ride a bike. All she wanted to do was to stop him from cutting down the tree. She didn't want to socialize or go to any parties. She had piles of paperwork to do. Besides the research, she was also editing a pamphlet on the Missions of the Bay Area.

"No problem. Swimming is not required. In fact, most of the women I know don't want to get their hair wet. But schmoozing is required. You do schmooze, don't you?" He was leaning so far over the fence, she could see the laugh lines around his eyes and the stubble of beard on his chin.

"I'm not sure," she said, taking a step backward. "In any case, I won't be schmoozing today. At the risk of sounding like a broken record, I have work to do."

"It's Saturday," he said. "Don't tell me you have to work all day."

"Wait a minute. Don't sound so shocked. You said entertaining was part of your work. So you're working on Saturday, too."

He held up his hand. "Touché," he said.

"I love my work," she said, and turned to go. Besides, she didn't know how much longer she could be exposed to his bare chest without staring as if she'd never seen a half-naked man before. He was having an unsettling effect on her. It must be that she hadn't had her coffee yet.

"That's what your aunt said about you," he said.

I'll bet she did, Sarah thought. I bet she told you all about me. Aunt Mary might have even told him she needed to go to a party with a bunch of people she didn't know so she could expand her horizons. Funny how people always seemed to think they knew what was best for you. Her parents sure did. They had hovered over her for years, giving advice and checking up on her daily even after she'd left home and had a life of her own.

Sarah loved her aunt dearly, but why couldn't she see that she was doing just fine the way she was? She turned back to face him. "Did she also tell you I'm here to keep an eye on you?"

"Can't keep an eye on me from over there at your house. You'd better come to the party or I'll have to come and get you." He grinned at her which annoyed her.

"I'll think about it," she said firmly, and this time she made it back to the house without a backward look. But even then, she couldn't shake the view she'd had of his tanned torso, quizzical gaze and granite jaw.

Yes, he was some hunk of man. If her aunt had mentioned that, she hadn't heard it. And if she had, she wouldn't have done anything differently. She hadn't drooled over him, she'd merely confronted him about mutilating the tree. Hopefully she could last the week without another run-in. One thing was for sure, she had no intention of going to his party. She looked forward to a long, peaceful afternoon immersed in another century.

Max stood at the fence, absently scratching his jaw, watching Sarah walk across the lawn, shoulders back, hips swaying gently under those baggy pants. It was her. Sleeping Beauty. Only not such a beauty behind those awful glasses and that oversize T-shirt. He was torn between immediately blurting out what had happened last night and keeping his mouth shut for the moment. Sooner or later he'd have to tell her. It looked like it was going to be later.

She was certainly an unusual type, even without the sleepwalking. Ms. Plain by day, a beauty by night. Definitely not his type. But then who was, these days? He hadn't had a girlfriend for almost two years, and he wasn't looking for one.

He had firsthand knowledge of how a seemingly perfect marriage could go sour and ruin the lives of not only the couple, but everyone else around, including children, friends and extended family. His parents' marriage had shown him that, and he wouldn't wish it on anyone.

Anybody with his job would naturally be discouraged from getting serious about anyone. Sure there were divorce lawyers who were married. Most of them married more than once. Who needed that kind of complication in their life? Alimony payments, recriminations. Unfair settlements. Child custody battles. Not for him. He saw enough of it. He wanted no part of it in his personal life.

Which was why he avoided serious relationships. Casual affairs, good times…sure. As long as both sides were consenting and had no unrealistic expectations, why not? But after the train wrecks he'd seen in divorce court, the fights, the broken homes and broken hearts, marriage was definitely not for him.

The way it was, his time was his own. His choices were his own. No compromises. No tears. No tantrums. No sleepless nights. He was a lucky man.

Chapter Two

Max knew full well what it was like to work on Saturday and Sunday, too. He'd teased Sarah, but she'd nailed him when she accused him of working today, too. He found his job challenging and he didn't mind working on weekends at all. He hadn't gotten where he was by slacking off. If he wanted to stay where he was, which was on top of the game, he had to work twice as hard as the others.

He got plenty of repeat business, which was a sad commentary on marriage, but when his clients turned to him to help out with the next settlement, he was there for them. Today he'd invited everyone he'd represented in the past few years. Some were good friends, some just clients. Some were remarried, some single, and some soon to be single.

Now that he thought about it, he didn't even know why he'd bothered to invite Sarah to his party. She wouldn't fit in and she probably wouldn't have a good time. So it was a good thing that she wasn't likely to show up. It was only that her aunt had not so subtly suggested she needed to get out more. And after last night, he felt he should keep an eye on her. Also he felt bad about waking her up this morning. After a night of sleepwalking, she needed her rest.

Max wondered if Sarah could remember what happened. The walking, the gathering of nuts, or the kiss? No, of course not. She would have said something. Or given some kind of sign. A look, a frown or a smile. He couldn't get over how different she looked. And yet there was a hint of that beautiful creature of the night in the way she held her head, the look in her eyes. It was maddening how elusive it was, there for a brief moment, and then gone again.

He hadn't realized until this morning how the tree was shading his pool, and he wanted to get out and do something before the party. Anything but worry about the few unhappy clients who felt they deserved more than they'd gotten in their settlements, and were blaming not only their ex, but him, too. It was a gut-wrenching business, dealing with people who'd failed while participating in one of life's most important unions, and it was sometimes depressing, but somebody had to do it and the proceeds had enabled him to enjoy the kind of lifestyle he'd once only dreamed of.

But there was pressure to keep it up. Today was the day to thank his clients with his yearly party, show off his new house, and do some general PR for himself. He really didn't need an extra woman there. One who'd stand out from all the others. He could hear the comments now.

"Who's the lady in the glasses? The one standing over there by herself."

"Doesn't look like one of Max's clients."

"Or one of his girlfriends."

"Where'd she come from?"

They hadn't seen her in the middle of the night. They had no idea how she looked in a sheer nightgown. He felt his pulse kick up a notch just thinking about it. He was sorry he'd invited her, because he definitely didn't want her at his party. Oh, well, she probably wouldn't come. So why worry?

His cell phone rang and he took it out of his back pocket. It was the caterer. They'd be setting up at three and were checking on the facilities at his house. Large oven, microwave, freezer space? Yes, yes and yes.

But when they came that afternoon in their white van with Countryside Catering painted on the side, they said they'd understood he had a double oven. He looked around the spotless, unused kitchen and wondered if he'd told them he had. Since he'd moved in a month ago, he really hadn't used the kitchen and he probably never would. He usually ate out or ordered in, so the kitchen was terra incognito.

While some of the crew set up tables on the spacious patio and started a barbecue going behind the house, others took over the kitchen, mixing salads, arranging appetizer puffs on baking sheets. Max wandered outside and looked across the fence. No sign of his neighbor. She was probably inside buried under a pile of history books. It was better that way. She wouldn't fit in with the group. He knew it and she probably knew it, too.

When he first saw her this morning he realized she was exactly what he'd expected from her aunt's description. And the complete opposite of the exotic creature of last night. Then the longer he stood there the more he was aware of her dual personality and changeable looks. He couldn't help wondering if she'd walk every night. Did he hope she'd wander in a see-through nightgown every night? Of course not. Now that he knew who she was. But what if she went somewhere else in her sheer nightgown? Down the street? Out into the street? That was a scary thought. He'd have to go after her. And he had to tell her. Or did she already know?

He also wondered if he was exactly what she'd expected from him. Or hadn't her aunt bothered to say anything about him except to warn her about the tree? It didn't matter. If he laid off the chain saw he wouldn't see her again, unless she walked at night or… No, he was convinced she wouldn't come to the party. Why should she? She didn't know anyone. She didn't even know him. Not as well as he knew her.

One of the caterers came out to the backyard, wiping her hands on her white apron.

"Mr. Monroe, it's almost four and we have to have another oven."

"Sorry about that, but that's all I've got."

She glanced across the fence. "What about using your neighbor, Mrs. Jenkins' oven? We catered a party there a little while back. Nice lady. I'm sure she wouldn't mind."

"No, she wouldn't, but she's not home." Too bad he'd gotten off on the wrong foot with Ms. History Buff by waking her up this morning and trying to reconcile her nocturnal self with her daytime persona, and he sure didn't make up for it by inviting her to his party. She'd made that clear. It was probably the last place she'd want to be this afternoon. But why not? Would it hurt her to put in an appearance? Lots of people went to parties where they didn't know anyone. That was the point. You went to meet new people. Why did he care? He didn't. Well, maybe just a little. Okay, he wanted to see her again. He wanted to see how she'd look dressed for a party. Somewhere between her sleepwalker nightgown and her baggy shorts, he imagined.

Why shouldn't she drop in, say hello, look around, and slip away if she was bored? It was a great day, there'd be fabulous food—if he could borrow her oven—and some attractive people there, though given her scholarly interests, she might find some of them on the shallow side.

"She's got someone house-sitting," he said. "I'll go ask her." She could always say no.

In answer to his knocking, she came to the back door, this time wearing a pair of elastic-waist shorts and the same T-shirt. Clearly she was not in a party mood. She was carrying a large book in one hand, no big surprise, and looking owlish behind those glasses.

"Yes?" she said disdainfully, as if he was a door-to-door salesman or someone handing out religious pamphlets.

"Hi. Remember me, your next-door neighbor?" he said cheerfully. He didn't wait for an answer. "I hate to bother you, but it's about my party, I think I mentioned I was having a party? Well, the caterers need an extra oven. It wouldn't take long, but they're baking these… I'm not sure what they are, but they'd sure appreciate it if they could use your oven for a little while. Unless you're using it," he added.

"No, I'm not. I guess it would be all right," she said doubtfully.

"That's great. I'll send them over. Thanks." He reached out and shook her hand, the one that wasn't clutching the book to her chest. "Your hands are cold," he said. "You should come outside in the sun."

"I can't, I'm…"

"Working, I know, but you can't stay inside on a day

like this. It's a crime against nature. I still expect you to drop in at the party. You can spare a few minutes, half hour at least, can't you?"

"Maybe," she said. In this case, that "maybe" sure sounded like a no.

He shrugged and told himself to forget it. Forget her. Hadn't she made it perfectly clear she did not want any part of his party?

An hour later, the hot appetizers were sizzling, thanks to Sarah's oven. The three-piece band was playing mariachi music and the bartender was making margaritas. His guests were tanned and reeking of ambition and money. Many were desperately seeking someone new to share their lives with, despite their past failures, but they all seemed to be having a good time. Sometimes Max worried about that desperation he saw on their faces.

He almost wanted to say, *Slow down, take it easy. Give it a rest. There are worse things than being alone. Being single has its advantages. And if you do get married again, don't rush into anything.*

But would they listen to him, their divorce lawyer? What did he know about wedded bliss? He knew plenty about the pain of divorce. *Their* divorces. Was he such a sterling example of single happiness? He thought so. They probably didn't.

He worked his way through the crowd, keeping his counsel to himself, making small talk and occasionally casting a glance across the fence. Wondering if the music penetrated the walls of her house or if she'd tuned everything out to concentrate.

He told himself to forget about her. Sure, she looked like something out of a fairy tale in the middle of the night. But by day, she was prickly and studious. She wasn't his type and she wasn't his responsibility. She wasn't even his neighbor. He would have had better luck inviting her outgoing and sociable aunt. He didn't mind escorting the niece back to bed if she came onto his property in the middle of the night, but a daytime party was a different matter.

He knew she really didn't want to come, and he also knew if she did, she'd feel out of place. He'd done his duty last night and today he'd invited her over. Her aunt hinted she needed a social life, but he couldn't force it on her. What did her aunt expect, that he'd drag her niece out of her house, force her to drink some tequila and do a Mexican hat dance? If she were here, her aunt would say, as any normal person would, "Good job, Max. The ball is in her court now. You've done everything you could and more. Don't worry about her."

He wasn't worried about her. He'd almost forgotten about her. But when Sarah finally appeared, he almost dropped his drink, he was so surprised. He set his glass down, waved and beckoned to her, afraid she'd change her mind when she saw the kind of people who were there. He shook his head slightly at the sight of her in a buttoned-up-to the neck, simple blue dress and low-heeled shoes. She always surprised him.

She couldn't be any more different from the rest of the crowd. She looked like she was on her way to the office. Or to an afternoon tea. She should have just kept on her shorts and T-shirt. She would have fit in better. As it was, she stood out like the proverbial sore thumb. The other women were wearing strapless stretch tops with bare midriffs showing above short shorts or cropped pants and tiny T-shirts whether they had the figure for it or not.

She looked so apprehensive she might have been facing the lion's den. And when she saw that he'd seen her, she had a trapped look in her eyes that said she knew she couldn't escape. He couldn't remember when he'd had that effect on a woman before. Why had she taken an instant dislike to him?

Did she wake up last night and realize what had happened? If she did, and she knew what had happened, she wasn't letting on, and she was a good actress. Or was it just the tree trimming that had turned her off? Had her aunt said something about him to discourage her? He'd like to know what it was.

He opened the gate in the fence between their houses and called to her. She forced a smile.

"I have to thank you for the use of your oven. I don't know what we would have done without it."

"You're welcome," she said.

"Come on in," he said. "They won't bite."

"These are your friends?" she asked, stepping onto his patio. He caught a whiff of some floral fragrance. So she cared enough to put some perfume on. And she'd brushed her brown hair so that it hung straight and shiny to her shoulders. She wasn't even wearing her glasses. She resembled the mysterious Sleeping Beauty a little more than she had this morning. He didn't know her at all, but he sensed that coming to a party with a lot of strangers was a big effort for her. Her aunt would be pleased. Too bad she couldn't have a good time while she was at it.

"Mostly business acquaintances."

"What do you do?"

"I'm a divorce lawyer."

"How sad. So everyone here is divorced?"

"Some have remarried since I represented them."

She looked around the patio. "It must be depressing, dealing in human misery."

He bristled at the remark because there was a grain of truth in it. But he was proud of his success. "I don't think of it that way," he said evenly. He personally didn't wreck anyone's home or break up anyone's marriage. He deliberately stayed away from any commitment. He did his best for his clients and he didn't like her thinking he took advantage of other people's misery. "The way I look at it, I'm the one who gets them out of their misery. Have you every been married?"

She shook her head. "Have you?"

"No."

"I can see why."

"Because of my thinning hair, my bloodshot eyes, my bowed legs?" he teased.

She blushed and let her gaze slide from his face then down to his Top-Siders, as if she was trying to decide what really had prevented him for getting married. "No, I mean you must get discouraged dealing with divorces all day. No wonder you haven't taken the plunge yourself. All those bitter people out there. If I were you, I'd avoid marriage also."

"Why have you?" he asked.

"I...I...I haven't met the right person," she said, shifting her gaze to the guests.

"Tell me," he said, "do these people look bitter to you?" They might be bitter, but he thought they put up a pretty good front.

People were laughing, men were tossing a beach ball back and forth across the pool, a few women were dangling their legs in the shallow end of the pool, while others were tossing down exotic drinks, and some couples were even nuzzling on colorful chaise lounges.

"I guess not. They actually look pretty happy. I'm sure that's thanks to you. You got them out of a bad situation into something better."

"That's how I look at it, otherwise…"

She looked at him as if waiting expectantly for him to finish his sentence. As if she really wanted to know. Otherwise, what would he do? He was a divorce lawyer, one of the best. He was in demand. And he would be as long as he did his job and got his clients large settlements. What would he do if he didn't think he'd improved his clients' situation? He met her gaze, looked into her clear blue eyes and answered her as firmly as he could. "Otherwise I wouldn't be able to sleep at night," he said.

She looked away and a tiny frown line appeared between her fine eyebrows. When he mentioned sleep, did it trigger some memory of last night? Did she wonder if she'd had an episode? Did she remember anything?

"Well," she said, brushing her hands together as if to dismiss any worries, either his or hers. "Don't let me keep you from your schmoozing."

When she said that, he realized he'd been talking to her exclusively for a long time and hadn't noticed what was going on behind him at the party. Not that anyone else had missed him. Just a glance told him that his guests were milling and mixing and generally amusing themselves. They didn't even miss him.

"I'd better get back to the guests. Come on, let me introduce you…"

"I can introduce myself."

He shot her a quick look. "Okay." But he thought it wasn't likely she'd go up to strangers. More likely she'd stand around and sneak back to her house when he wasn't looking.

Before he could make the rounds, his cell phone rang and he went inside to give directions to someone who couldn't find the house. He stood by the open

French doors looking out at the party scene, his eyes glued to Sarah. She was standing at the edge of the pool, talking to an old college buddy of his whose divorce had been finalized last month.

He had to say, in her dress and pale skin, she stood out like an English rose in the middle of a tropical garden. Of all the women there, she was refreshingly different. Frisbees sailed through the air, couples danced on the patio to the live music and a beach ball bounced off the diving board and into the deep end.

Suddenly there was a scream and a splash and he went running out to the pool. There was Sarah flailing about in the deep end, her head sinking under the water, her hair trailing behind her.

"Call 911," he yelled. Then Max jumped into the water to save her.

Chapter Three

They say your whole life passes in front of you when you think you're going to die, but all Sarah could think of as the water closed over her head and she began sinking to the bottom of the pool, was that she should have worn nicer underwear, instead of those white cotton granny underpants and sports bra. Which was stupid, because the coroner wasn't going to notice, but the man next door might.

And then she thought of her parents, who'd say, *What were you doing even close to a swimming pool! You know what could happen.*

Then everything went black.

The next thing she knew she was lifted out of the water and propped up on cool blue tiles. She gasped for breath, coughing and spitting out water. She reached for her inhalator, but it wasn't there. She'd left it at home. Max was leaning towards her, his face blurred, his eyebrows drawn together.

People were shouting.

"What happened?"

"Who is she?"

"Where are the paramedics?"

"Is she alive?"

"Does anyone know CPR?"

"Give her mouth-to-mouth."

Her heart pounded. Until she realized it wasn't an asthma attack. Even though she was choking and scared, she had enough presence of mind to know she didn't need an inhalator and resuscitation wasn't necessary. All she needed was a few minutes to expel the water out of her lungs and she'd be fine. She was proud of herself. She didn't panic.

Someone patted her on the back and she coughed water into Max's face. He didn't flinch. Blurry-eyed, she looked around at a dozen faces staring down at her, who were all looking scared, and some downright terrified. She wished she could reassure them, but she couldn't speak. Even more she wanted to sink down into oblivion. She wished she'd never come to this party. She hated being the center of attention. Memories of schoolmates staring at her during an asthma attack, of being sent to the school nurse came flooding back. She was conscious of her dress plastered to her body, her hair hanging in wet strands. The humiliation was almost worse than drowning.

"What happened?" she gasped.

"You got knocked into the pool," a man's voice came from somewhere behind her. "Sorry about that. I didn't see you standing there when I jumped in. How are you?"

She nodded. "I'm fine. I think I'll just…" Just nothing. She tried to get up, but couldn't, so she put her head between her knees and her eyes filled with tears. Tears of relief, and of mortification. She couldn't move or speak. She wished everyone would go away and let her recover on her own.

It was Max who pulled her up by her arms and lifted her to her wobbly feet. "I'll take her home. She lives next door. Send the paramedics over there."

"I really don't need…" She really didn't need anything, no paramedics, no mouth-to-mouth, just a few minutes to pull herself together. God, she hated it when people made a fuss over her. She wanted to seem cool, calm and collected but a long series of racking coughs spoiled the effect.

Max carried her home, her face pressed against his chest, her legs dangling over his arm. She wanted to tell him she could walk, but she couldn't seem to get the words out. She tried to wriggle out of his grasp, but she didn't have the strength, so she just let herself go limp. He felt so big and so strong and she felt so small and ridiculously safe in his arms. For a person who prided herself on her hard-won independence, it was a troubling moment laced with conflicting emotions.

Being taken care of was better than she cared to admit. On the other hand, she hated having to depend on anyone. To her surprise, without her instructions, he walked into the kitchen and up the stairs of her aunt's house, as if he knew exactly where the bedroom was. Just inside the door, he tried to unbutton her wet dress while still holding her.

"I can do it," she mumbled, but her own fingers were clumsy and even shakier than his and she gave up. "It's okay," she said. "Leave it."

"Can't leave you in a wet dress," he muttered. So he didn't. He set her on the edge of the bed and yanked at the buttons until they popped off, and pulled her wet dress over her head. Wearing only her wet underwear, she quickly slid under the covers to hide her too thin body and her too sensible underwear before he could see any more than he already had.

It was all too awful. She closed her eyes hoping Max would go away. Of course he didn't. He stood at the door with his arms crossed over his chest, dripping water on the carpet. Was he the one who'd pulled her out of the pool? Her mind was a blank.

Before she could ask, a pair of burly emergency technicians stomped up the stairs, barged into the room and flipped back the quilt to check her out. She wanted to curl up and play dead. She didn't know where Max was at that moment. Had he stepped out of the room out of consideration for her modesty? What did it matter? He'd already seen her in next to nothing.

The men took her pulse, her blood pressure, looked in her mouth and listened to her lungs and her heart, while she assured them in no uncertain terms that she was fine. If they'd taken her temperature, they might have thought she had a fever, but in reality her body only burned with red-hot embarrassment.

They asked her a lot of questions, and she answered them in a voice that was not really hers. The answers must have been satisfactory because they turned and spoke in low tones to someone else, probably Max, who apparently was still in the room.

She hated to be treated like she was sick. It reminded her of her childhood, of the asthma attacks, the trips to the emergency room, being carried into the steam-filled bathroom in the middle of the night and her ever-present inhaler tucked into her backpack at school, just in case. She thought she was over that. As long as she didn't overexert, she could lead a normal life. As long as she stuck to studying California's history and didn't venture into other people's parties. She led a very satisfying life. Until now.

Even worse than being treated like an invalid, she discovered, was being treated like she wasn't there. The paramedic team in the room discussed her situation, debated whether to prescribe anything and in general carried on like she was in a coma. "Excuse me. I'm not unconscious," she said. "I'm alive and well. I should tell you I have asthma, but it's under control."

They turned to look at her as surprised as if a statue

had spoken. They took notes, wrote on a chart and after an eternity, the paramedics left and she was propped up against her aunt's small embroidered pillow shams. She'd quietly shed her underwear and hidden them under the sheets, and now she wore nothing but a comforter pulled up to her chin. She glared at the man who was standing at the foot of her bed. Why was he still there? She was fine. She'd been poked and prodded and lectured to and she was exhausted. But fine.

"How are you feeling?" Max asked, his eyebrows drawn together in concern.

"Fine, thank you." *Now go.*

"I don't know what happened, but…"

"I got knocked in the water, that's all. At least that's what the man said. My fault. I wasn't watching and I was standing too close to the edge. No big deal. I didn't drown. Thanks to you. I don't know how to thank you enough. You saved my life."

"It was nothing. But you'll have to learn to swim."

"Or stay away from pools."

"I can teach you."

"That's very nice, but…"

"Tomorrow."

Max was still reeling from the close brush she'd had with disaster. His hands were shaking and his heart was pounding, but that could have something to do with seeing Sarah in her underwear. He got the message when she closed her eyes indicating as clearly as possible that she'd had enough of him and being fussed over, and then pointed to the door. He backed out of the room before he had a chance to ask if she wanted him to find her nightgown, that same gauzy white nightgown he'd seen her in last night. He wouldn't mind seeing her again in or out of it. But he knew when he wasn't wanted.

Maybe if she wore the nightgown again, she might remember what had happened last night. Maybe then they'd get it out in the open and he could ask her if she had a problem, or if she knew she had a problem.

He also wanted to know why a California girl didn't know how to swim. Was it just because she had asthma? Lots of athletes had it. Sure, it was a problem, but not an insurmountable one. He wondered how she could think of an excuse for not learning to swim now that she lived next door to a pool, and most particularly he wanted to know why he shouldn't teach her. One thing for sure. After today, he couldn't have her living so close by when she couldn't swim. Especially if she made any more unexpected visits to his house in the middle of the night. Despite the fence-enclosed pool with the locked gate, it was too dangerous and it was his responsibility to teach her, whether she wanted to learn or not.

When he got back to the party, the atmosphere had changed. There was a pall hanging over the gathering. The music continued, but no one was dancing. The guests were no longer playing games around the pool. It was as if they'd been frozen in place until he returned and assured everyone that his neighbor was fine, that no one was to blame.

Personally he thought it was possible the guests had been imbibing too much, playing ball and jumping around the pool in a careless way. They were his clients, not his friends, if that was any consolation to him. They weren't all people he'd hang out with if he hadn't handled their divorces. On the other hand, why didn't she know how to swim? He was going to rectify that starting tomorrow.

The party went on for just a short time. The margaritas were still available, the food was still plentiful, but a few people had left and others were saying goodbye, as if they'd been waiting for his report before taking off, and were now blowing air kisses all around.

He was just as glad. He'd had enough of schmoozing, enough of empty chatter and pretending everything was fine. He couldn't get Sarah out of his mind. She'd looked so vulnerable, felt so fragile in his arms, but back in her room she'd bounced back, and had been well enough to order him out. She had guts. Imagine being pushed into a pool when you couldn't swim and recovering so fast. At least he thought she'd recovered. At soon as everyone left, he'd go back and make sure she was okay.

But when he knocked on her back door an hour later, there was no answer. He let himself in, walked up the stairs and stood in the doorway. She was lying on her side, and breathing evenly. He heaved a sigh of relief.

It was dusk, but from the pale beams of the night-light, he could see her face was flushed, her eyelashes shadowing her cheek. He stood there for a long moment, the faint smell of eucalyptus in the air. Oh, yes, the nuts from the tree on her bedside table. He picked them up and inhaled the fragrance. Hadn't she noticed? Hadn't she wondered how they'd gotten there?

He was jarred by the ringing of her phone.

He raced down the stairs and grabbed the phone from the kitchen wall. Maybe it was her aunt.

"I'm calling for Sarah," said a woman's voice.

"She's uh…can I take a message?"

"Who's this?"

"A neighbor."

"I see. You can tell her her mother called. Just checking to see how she is."

"She's fine."

"Where is she?"

"She's here, but she's asleep."

"Asleep? It's only eight o'clock."

"If it's urgent, I can wake her."

"No, no, it's all right. What did you say your name was?"

Max grinned. A strange man answering the phone. Her daughter asleep. No wonder she was worried.

"Max," he said. "I live next door. I'll tell her you called."

"Thank you."

He hung up, wrote a note for Sarah and left it on her

kitchen counter. Then he went home and sat on his patio, smoking a cigar and thinking. If she walked tonight, he wanted to be there.

Chapter Four

The phone rang shrilly and wakened Sarah with a start for the second morning in a row. This time she knew exactly where she was. What she didn't know was who would be calling her at seven on a Sunday morning. She felt groggy and very naked, the 300-count cotton sheets brushing against her bare skin every time she moved. It was all so strange and unfamiliar. Then it all came back. The pool, the accident, the water, the party and Max. She clutched the sheet to her chest before picking up the phone.

"Sarah, is anything wrong?" her mother asked.

Nothing's wrong, I almost drowned, that's all. She could just imagine her mother's overreaction to that. "Of course not, why are you calling so early?" She was aware of how crabby she sounded, but couldn't control herself. It was all those years of being coddled. She couldn't take it anymore. She was a grown-up, on her own. It was time to put a stop to it.

"I called last night and a strange man answered the phone. He said you were asleep."

"That's right. I was. I went to bed early." But why did a strange man answer the phone? Max. That's who it was. Why had he answered her phone? "And the strange man? Nobody you know. Just Aunt Mary's next door neighbor paying a neighborly visit."

"Are you sure you're all right? You always get up early."

"I have to go now, Mom." She searched her brain for an excuse to hang up. Then, instead of shielding her mother from the truth, she said boldly, "I have a swimming lesson today."

"A swimming lesson?" Her mother's voice rose in alarm the way she knew it would. "You don't swim. You can't do sports. It's too risky."

"I know I don't swim. That's the problem. It's about time I learned. It's about time I took some risks."

"But Sarah…"

Warning bells rang. Echoes of the past. Her mother's voice.

You can't swim.

Mustn't run.

Don't go out.

Stay home.

Indoors.

You're different. Not like other kids.

Sarah took a deep breath. "I haven't had an attack for months, no years. I'm fine. It's time I made some changes in my life." Nothing drastic, of course. Just a swimming lesson. A vision of her volunteer swimming teacher came to mind. The man with the gray eyes and mouthwatering body. Imagining him in the pool with her. Her mouth went dry. With shaking hands, she reached for the glass of water on her bedside stand.

Maybe he hadn't meant it. Maybe he was just worried she'd sue him for negligence. Maybe… Enough maybes. Just her mother's admonition was enough to make up her mind. She was over twenty-five years old. Her asthma was under control. Oh, she'd never be like everyone else. But she could come a little closer.

Her parents were still worried about her. Their concern made her feel claustrophobic. Which made her feel guilty. They loved her. They doted on her. But she was too old to be doted on. She would take a swimming lesson. She might not be able to learn how to swim at her advanced age, but by heaven, she'd try.

"Got to run now Mom. I have to buy a swimsuit." She hung up quickly before her mother could start in again.

When she returned from the mall with a two-tone suit, a white terry cover-up and a pedicure, she wasn't quite sure what to do next. Change into her suit and knock on Max's door? Lean over the fence and see where he was? Go back to work and wait for him to make another offer?

While she was thinking it over, she put the suit on and stood in front of Aunt Mary's full-length mirror. She frowned at her reflection. Why had she let the saleswoman talk her into anything with a low neckline and high-cut legs? She sure didn't look like anyone who was at the party yesterday. All those beautiful people turning bronze under the hot sun. In contrast, she was white and skinny. All the more reason to get out and absorb some Vitamin D, right?

No time like the present. Before she could change her mind, she wrapped herself in her terry cover-up, poured herself a glass of lemonade, grabbed a big straw hat from her aunt's closet and her book on the California rancheros and headed outside to Aunt Mary's hammock. Before she faced anyone, including her neighbor, she might even take off her hat and robe and get a little color in her cheeks so she didn't look so anemic.

She glanced across the fence, but all was quiet at Max's house. No sound. No movement. She felt a little letdown, for no reason at all. The plan was to get outside into the elements and absorb a few rays before she saw him again. Of course she might not see him again. Ever.

Maybe he offered to help every woman he met. Just a reflex action on his part. She really knew nothing about the handsome neighbor, except for what he did for a living. She couldn't believe he had to deal with failure every day in his work. No matter what he said about it, it had to have an effect on his psyche. On the other hand, he must be good at it to be able to afford to live where he did. Maybe that's all he cared about. The money.

The sun was warm. The air was still. Sarah stretched her legs out in front of her and studied her startlingly bright red toenails, wondering what had possessed her to do something so out of character. Then she read a few pages about Secundino Robles, a handsome blue-eyed native Californio who was the Don Juan of his day in the nineteenth century, sweeping many eager young settler women off their feet. Her eyes grew heavy. She closed the book. The hammock rocked gently.

When she woke from a dream about a romantic swash-buckling cowboy who spent his life racing around the countryside visiting brothels, cantinas and gambling houses, the sun was low in the sky. Her skin felt prickly and her mouth was dry. Not only that, but she felt like she'd been intimately involved with one of those cowboys.

What was so amazing was that he looked a little bit like the man next door, with his gray eyes, broad shoulders and all. And oh yes, a wide-brimmed cowboy hat. She pressed her hand against her heart to see if it was really beating so fast. It was. Ridiculous. It was just a dream. Such adventurous men didn't exist in today's world. If they did, she hadn't met any.

Once again she felt a sense of displacement. She

looked around for a long moment, lost in another century, where wild men on stolen horses carried loaded flintlocks, and ardently pursued women who flirted shamelessly and definitely without their parents' approval from behind rawhide window coverings.

She often dreamed about the past. Especially when she was in the middle of a project. But she'd never had erotic dreams before, never felt the dreams were so real. Or the men were so real.

She shook her head to try to clear it. She was not a damsel in love with a caballero. Only a twenty-first century history buff who lived most of the time in another world. Today she'd done something completely out of character. Besides buying a swimsuit and getting a pedicure, she'd taken a nap for once in her life. She never napped in hammocks or anywhere else for that matter. On the other hand, she never fell into swimming pools, either. She'd never been rescued before or pursued by a dashing horse thief. She wasn't the type to inspire that kind of bravado. But she'd been saved yesterday from a watery accident and she'd been carried off by her swashbuckling neighbor. That much was real.

But that was yesterday. Today he was nowhere to be seen. She yawned and got up out of the hammock. Still no activity in the yard next door. So he hadn't really meant to help her. She'd bought a swimsuit for nothing. She felt cold and empty. She needed a cup of tea, that's all, not a swimming lesson.

She wrapped her terry robe tightly around her and headed for her house. Even barefoot, her feet felt heavy. She told herself to get back to real life. She was out of her league and she didn't know how to play games. Nor did she want to learn. The kind of people at her neighbor's party were not the kind of people she wanted to know.

Before she reached her door, she glanced casually toward the house next door. There he was, leaning against the redwood fence, arms crossed, with a grin on his face as if he'd been there for hours watching her. She stopped in her tracks and stared at him.

"Hey, Sleeping Beauty," Max called. "Where've you been? Come on over. It's time for your lesson."

"How…how long have you been standing there?" she asked, clutching her robe tightly around her waist.

"Not long. I didn't say anything because I didn't want to wake you." He flung the gate open and stood there waiting. He was bare-chested for the second day in a row, impossibly good-looking in a pair of drawstring swim shorts. She swallowed hard and averted her gaze.

What could she do? Follow her instincts and run into her aunt's house? Make up an excuse or say she'd changed her mind? The one thing she couldn't do was to tell the truth and say she'd lost her nerve. That she was afraid, not so much of the water, although that was a problem, but of having him hold her up in the water and watch her flail around helplessly, gasping for breath and sputtering like yesterday. The memories of kids on the playground staring at her when she'd have an asthma attack, then turning their heads and shunning her would always be a part of her past. If she struggled in the water, and of course she would, then he'd know for sure what an incompetent, nonathletic wimp she really was. The good thing was he'd never guess she'd dreamed about him. No, not really him, someone else who looked like him but came from another era.

He'd seen her stripped down, without her clothes, he knew she couldn't swim, but he had no idea how inept she was at anything physical. He must realize how different she was from the people at his party with their muscles and tans? Or how far apart her world was from theirs? Of course. It must be obvious.

She was making too much of this. It was a swimming lesson. That's all. One lesson. She could handle it. And if she couldn't, she could leave. He was only doing it to be nice. As a favor to Aunt Mary. As soon as he realized how truly dorky she was, how uncoordinated and unaccustomed to physical activities, he'd give up, give in and let her go back to her world, the world of books, the world of long ago.

She pasted a smile on her lips and walked through the gate, brushing past him in her fluffy robe, getting a tantalizing whiff of some elusive male scent like citrus aftershave. She tossed her robe onto a deck chair as if she'd been doing it all her life, and sat on the edge of the pool where the water was about three feet deep.

Then she turned her head in his direction, determined to go through with this. After all, yesterday she'd nearly drowned. She couldn't let that happen again.

"Never had a swim lesson?" he asked.

She shook her head.

"We're even," he said. "I've never given one."

This was her chance. Get up gracefully and say thanks, but no thanks. She could even make up a story about signing up for swim lessons at the YWCA in town. But before she could move a muscle or say a word, he'd jumped in the water and was standing in front of her, his skin smooth and wet, looking up at her, with his hands covering hers. His eyelashes were wet, his eyes gleamed silver in the fading sunlight. She shivered with anticipation. She couldn't learn to swim. Not from him. Not from someone who looked like George Clooney.

"Cold? The water's warmer than the air. Come on in." He tugged at her wrists and she gave in and slid into the water, feeling surprisingly graceful. With his hands still holding her wrists, he pulled her into slightly deeper water until her shoulders were covered. She swallowed hard, trying not to panic as the water lapped at her neck. He gave her a reassuring smile and she gripped his hands tightly.

He was right about one thing, the water was warmer than the air. And even though she was in deeper water than she'd ever been before, she felt strangely secure with him holding her hands. Until he made her put her head underwater. Then she felt her heart pound. It took her three tries before she could actually keep her head under for longer than two seconds and open her eyes to a blue, watery world.

He put his face under the water and grinned at her. Even distorted he was undeniably handsome in a rugged way. He made a face at her, wiggling his eyebrows and waving his hands. She laughed and choked and he scooped her up and carried her to the shallow end.

"You okay?" he asked.

"Of course," she insisted, realizing that this was the second time in two days he'd picked her up and carried her to safety. The second time in two days when he'd made her feel safe and protected. This time she had no excuse to throw her arms around his neck and bury her face against his chest. But she wanted to. Oh, yes, she'd be a liar if she didn't admit that she wanted to badly.

"You did great," he said, letting her slide out of his arms. "You're a natural."

She shook the water out of her ears. "A natural coward."

"No way. After what happened yesterday, most people wouldn't go near the water. Are you sure you've never taken lessons before?"

She ran one hand through her wet hair. "Flattery will get you anywhere. If I did well, it's because of you. Are you sure you've never taught swimming before?"

He shook his head and she turned to go, eyeing the deck of the pool and the gate and the safety of her aunt's house next door. She'd had a lesson. She'd gotten into the water. And she hadn't drowned. That was enough for one day. "Thanks."

"Wait a minute. We're just getting started."

She sighed. She should have known she couldn't get off so easily. The next thing she knew he had her floating on her back with his arms around her, supporting her body. She was afraid he'd let go, but more afraid of enjoying the sensation of his arms around her. The slightly scary sensation of being afloat in the water coupled with the excitement of his body so close to hers.

"Relax," he said.

"Easy for you to say," she muttered. How could she relax with one of his hands brushing the underside of her breasts and the other cupping her bottom. It was too intimate, too close, too terrifying. Then he wanted her to turn over and put her head in the water.

"I can't," she said, twisting her head to look him in the eye.

"Okay," he said, uprighting her gently, and brushing his hands together. "Lesson One is over. You're making great progress."

She straightened and planted her feet firmly on the turquoise pool bottom. "Great progress?" Despite the chills running up her spine, she chuckled. "Either you have low expectations, or you're a born cheerleader."

He grinned. "See you tomorrow. Lesson Two."

"Tomorrow?" she said faintly. "So soon? Don't you have to go to work?"

"If I can fit it into my schedule, so can you," he said.

"Right," she said, walked up the steps to the edge of the pool and grabbed her robe. "Thanks again."

"Wait," he said, still standing waist-deep in the water. "Your mother called last night. Did you get the message?"

"Yes, I did. She called me back this morning. I wish you hadn't answered the phone. Now she's curious. She wants to know who you are."

One corner of his mouth quirked in a smile. "What did you tell her?"

"The truth. That you're Aunt Mary's neighbor. I didn't want to tell my parents about my, uh, accident. I appreciate your keeping quiet, too. They'd only worry."

"They ought to feel better knowing you're learning to swim."

"Maybe they ought to, but they wouldn't. You don't know my parents," she muttered. "Worrying about me is their full-time job." She walked to the gate, unlatched it and turned. "Anyway, thanks again for the lesson." How many times had she thanked him? Why couldn't she just walk away without another glance at that handsome face and that mouthwatering body? Fascination. Male perfection. That was the answer. She was staring at him the way she would stare at a Greek statue. She'd have to be made of stone herself not to notice.

Only he was real. And so was she. She could still feel his hands on her skin.

"Till tomorrow," he said.

Chapter Five

Max watched her walk across his lawn and onto her aunt's property. She had a trim, cute little body, which he'd seen last night, of course, but hadn't taken advantage of the situation to really look at her while she was undressed. Now, watching her slender legs and her little butt sway gently as she walked, he stood and admired the view until she'd disappeared into Mary's house.

Damn, he'd meant to tell her about the sleepwalking. He couldn't let it go like this. Too dangerous. Maybe she knew. Maybe she didn't. In any case, he couldn't rest until he knew she knew and that she was going to do something about it. What that would be, he wasn't sure. Lock her doors? Set up an alarm system?

Sleep with a friend? He wondered if she had a friend to sleep with. She wasn't every man's cup of tea, exactly. It would take someone special to appreciate her bookish looks by day and her exotic looks by night. Either day or night, she had guts, he'd give her that.

Actually he'd give her more than that. First he'd shower and change and go over and take some of the leftover food from his party which was ample for another small feast. It would be a good excuse to see her again. Why did he need an excuse? Why did he want to see her again so soon? He refused to contemplate why. Luckily she'd be gone in a week. So what harm did it do to get to know her a little bit? After that, he'd never see her again.

Maybe she'd rather be alone, he thought, an hour later, as he knocked on her back door, with a heavy paper bag full of leftovers and, a bottle of wine. Or maybe she'd gone out. Maybe she was pretending she wasn't home. Maybe she'd had enough of him.

But whether she had or not, she finally came to the door, dressed in her usual baggy shirt and shapeless pants, her hair pulled back from her face and her eyes magnified by her huge steel-rimmed glasses.

"Oh," she said, "it's you."

"Were you expecting someone else?"

"No, but…"

"But you didn't know how neighborly life in the suburbs could be, did you? Neighbors attacking your tree, then dropping in, giving parties, invading your space and luring you to their swimming pool. Look, I'm probably interrupting, but I had so much food left over from my party, I thought maybe, if you haven't had dinner, you might like some grilled salmon and asparagus and mushroom turnovers and a glass of wine or two. I don't think you got a chance to eat much at the party yesterday."

She stood in the doorway looking flustered. "No, that's right, but, I couldn't possibly…" Was she ever going to invite him in? Didn't look that way. "Here," he said, holding out the paper bag.

"Would you like to come in?" she asked finally as he propped his foot in the door.

"I thought you'd never ask," he said.

He was in. He felt like pumping his fist in the air. Like it was a major triumph to be allowed to offer her a free, delicious dinner. She was the strangest woman he'd ever met. He really had no idea why he was there at all.

He'd never had to work so hard to share a dinner with someone. Was it him? Or would she be this way with anyone? It was enough to shake an ordinary man's confidence in himself. But Max was not an ordinary man and he was determined to get to the bottom of this woman's problem.

Maybe she hesitated because it wasn't her house. Or maybe she didn't want him there under any circumstances. He usually didn't get that reaction from women. Usually he was the one retreating, the one who was running from involvement. He was the one making up excuses. Was that really why he was there? Because she was a challenge? Sarah made it clear she wasn't thrilled to see him again. That bothered him for some reason. He wanted to know why. He thought they were getting along so well. Was it something her aunt had told her about him or did she just hate all divorce lawyers? Some people did.

It was too bad if Sarah didn't want him there. There was all this great food and wine, and he'd be damned if he'd eat it by himself. Not when her aunt has specifically asked him to look out for her. As if she'd read his mind, Sarah took the containers out of the bag and spread the food out on the kitchen table. Then she looked up at him.

"What did my aunt tell you about me?" she asked. Her nose was wrinkled as if bracing herself for the worst. She had a very cute nose, he noticed. Now if only she could get rid of the thick glasses and the baggy clothes. He knew she had nothing to hide. He'd seen her in her nightgown, in next to nothing after her fall into the pool, and in her swimsuit. She had great legs, a cute little butt, small but perfect breasts, all of which he'd had a chance to admire during her swimming lesson. He could hardly wait for the next opportunity for her to remove her clothes. And he'd only known her for two days.

He took a deep breath. He had to tell her. He had to tell her now.

"I'll tell you what she *didn't* tell me," he said.

She grabbed the wine bottle he'd brought and inserted the opener into the cork as if her life depended on it. As if she didn't want to hear what he was going to say. Did she suspect?She said nothing. She didn't even look at him. Wasn't she curious?

"That you sleepwalk," he said.

She set the bottle down with a bang and clapped her hand to her mouth. "Oh, no. I don't believe it."

"Yes. The night before last you came to my garden in your nightgown. You were asleep."

Her face flushed. She looked so distressed he wondered if he should have told her after all. "I'm so embarrassed. I thought I was over it."

"So it's happened before?"

"When I was a child. It wasn't bad enough I'd wake up choking and wheezing with asthma. Even when I was breathing normally and free from attacks, I'd sometimes get up in the night and rearrange the dolls in my room. When I woke up in the morning I didn't remember a thing. I thought they'd moved around on their own. They were so real to me. I don't think I ever left the house while sleeping or my parents would have panicked. But since I grew up, it's only happened a few times, when I'm in a new place, or under stress. What, uh, what did I do, where did I go?" she asked, her face pale.

"Nothing much. You were just wandering in my garden behind the house. Then you went home, with a little help from me."

"You took me home? Why didn't you say something to me?" she asked.

"I'd heard somewhere it's dangerous to wake the sleepwalker."

"I mean yesterday."

"I was waiting for the right opportunity. And just in case, I was watching your house last night. You didn't come outside."

"I don't know what to say," she said, biting her lower lip. "You've saved me twice in the space of two days."

"My pleasure," he said, pouring wine into a glass and handing it to her. "Oh, yes, while you were sleeping, you gathered some eucalyptus nuts from my tree on the ground behind my house."

She nodded slowly, her eyebrows drawn together in concentration. "The ones on the bedside table. I wondered how they got there. I love the smell. It's so pungent. The oil from the leaves is used to make medicine, you know. And the wood is useful, too, for lumber. The trees came from Australia. They call them Gum treess. The first mention of eucalyptus in California is in an article about a man named W. C. Walker who had a nursery in San Francisco and planted some eucalyptus seeds. It was 1850-something, no wait—" She broke off with a sheepish smile as if she was afraid she was boring him. "But that's probably more than you wanted to know about eucalyptus trees. I get carried away with history."

"You make it interesting."

"I hope so, because it is interesting to me. All the little details. But not to most people. I forget everyone doesn't share my fascination with the past. Some people call it an obsession. But there are some wonderful stories. I don't know when to stop, so you wouldn't want to get me started."

"Why not?"

"Because I love history and I could go on and on. Just drop a name or a famous place and I know how it got there. I get so wound up I can't resist telling the story until I've put everyone to sleep. That's why—" She stopped and sipped her wine thoughtfully.

"Anyway, back to my sleepwalking. It's not dangerous to wake a sleepwalker. That's a misconception. So if I ever do it again, I mean if you see me out gathering nuts in the middle of the night or any other activity, please wake me up."

"I will. I definitely will. Any suggestions?"

"Just give me a little shake or whatever."

"Whatever?" he asked. "There's a legend, isn't there, or is it a fairy tale? How does the prince wake Sleeping Beauty?" he asked, feigning innocence. He liked to see her blush. He liked watching her when she was caught off guard.

"Oh, uh, I don't know." She turned her back to him. Why didn't she just say he woke her with a kiss? Didn't she know or was she really that shy?

"Just in case," Sarah continued, "so you don't have to worry, I'm going to move downstairs to Aunt Mary's guest room and lock the doors at night. But now that I've settled in to her house, I'll be okay. Don't feel you have to stay outside watching for me." She laughed lightly as if it was a ridiculous idea, but he wasn't so sure, given the swimming pool incident.

"The gate to my pool is locked," he said, "in case you're worried. And I'm a night owl anyway, so if you do come, I'll see you and I'll be sure to wake you this time. If only I knew how the prince did it." He rubbed his chin and gave her an inquiring look as if he really needed to know.

She avoided his glance by opening a cabinet to take out some plates and then by carefully filling the salt and pepper shakers. Maybe she remembered that he'd kissed her. Maybe not. In any case, the word kiss had not come up. But he couldn't keep from staring at her lips, remembering, thinking, feeling that kiss.

"Thanks for helping me out," she said, turning her attention to the food he'd brought. "And thanks for all this. It looks wonderful." She set the table with brightly colored place mats and casual china with hand-painted flowers on it along with heavy silverware, but she had a faraway look in her eyes as if she was somewhere in history, thinking about something else, some other time.

"Look," he said, putting his hand on her arm, hoping to bring her back to the present. "I hope I did the right thing by telling you. I certainly didn't mean to worry you over nothing."

"Nothing?" she said, looking down at him with a

worried frown. "I was wandering in your yard. Trespassing. What if you hadn't been there to bring me home? What if I'd walked out into someone else's property?" Her forehead was creased with fine lines.

"But you didn't. From what you say, it's probably not going to happen again."

She nodded, but he couldn't tell if she was convinced. He divided the food onto their plates and was pleased to see her sit down across from him and start eating. As for him, it sure beat eating alone, he realized with a start. He usually ate dinner in front of the TV. He thought he didn't need anyone around on a regular basis. He didn't know the meaning of the word lonely. He probably didn't need anyone around on a regular basis. But just this once, it wasn't bad. Not bad at all. He watched her when she wasn't looking and she seemed to enjoy the food. If only for that, he was glad he'd come over tonight.

"This is very good," she said, as if she, too, was surprised at how pleasant it was to share dinner with someone. "I didn't know I was hungry. I just hope I didn't spoil your party yesterday." She set her fork on the table and looked earnestly into his eyes. He realized she'd taken off her glasses and her eyes were huge and expressive. Fascinating change. He couldn't tear his gaze away.

"You added a little drama, that's all. And it wasn't your fault. It was mine for allowing the atmosphere to deteriorate that way so that you got knocked in. Everyone was relieved to hear you were all right. You *are* all right, aren't you?"

"Fine. I feel like I'm completely recovered. I'm just having a little trouble concentrating. But that has nothing to do with falling into the pool. You see, I thought it would be good for me to get away from the office, but I didn't realize what a different world it is down here, and I wonder if I'm really going to get anything done after all."

"Would that be so bad if you took the week off and didn't get anything done but learning to swim?"

"Yes, it would. I have deadlines. I have projects. The people I work with expect a lot from me. My boss is great. And I can't let her down, especially when she's got personal problems. And we're in the middle of a fund-raising campaign for the Historical Society." She stopped for a moment. "In a week?" she asked, as if the words had just sunk in. "You think I could learn to swim in a week?"

He grinned. "Well, you might not qualify for the Olympics, but with my expert teaching methods, we might be able to make you water-safe."

Sarah smiled at his attempt at self-deprecating humor and nodded. He really was a nice guy after all. Besides being a bonafide hunk, and easy to look at across the table, he'd been thoughtful enough to bring her dinner. He didn't just leave it on the doorstep, he stayed to share it with her. She was having a good time. She thought he was, too. Besides all this, he was actually teaching her to swim. He'd gone out of his way to invite her to his party. The accident wasn't his fault. Maybe her aunt had encouraged him to be friendly, but he'd done it. And most of all, he'd brought her back home from sleepwalking.

Sleepwalking? She was shocked to hear about that. What next? She'd gotten over her asthma attacks only to find she'd taken up sleepwalking after all these years? Another thing to keep from her parents. She could just hear their cries of dismay. Their insistence that she move back to her apartment. That she not take chances.

"I'd like to be water-safe," she said, trying to forget her parents and putting her other problems aside for the moment. "As for taking the week off completely, I can't do that. Besides deadlines on the papers I'm writing for our society's publications, I'm giving a presentation next weekend at the society's annual meeting. With my boss out sick lately I've taken over some of the administrative stuff. If I hadn't promised Aunt Mary…"

"Wait a minute, you're not going to back out and go back home, are you? Just when you're making such headway in your swimming?"

"I'm not backing out," she assured him. "I'm sure by tomorrow I'll be able to get some work done on my paper and on my presentation. Also won't the neighborhood quiet down come Monday when everyone goes back to work?"

"Not if you're referring to me," he said. "Because I

work at home a lot, and I generally meet clients in the evening at their office or my home after work. But rarely on a Sunday. I promise I'll talk softly and even better, I won't touch my chain saw again, if that's what you're worried about."

"Let's see if I've got this straight. Aunt Mary warned me you were going to cut her tree down which isn't really true, so what did she tell you about me?" She held her breath, expecting the worst. Surely her aunt wouldn't have mentioned the asthma or Sarah's parents' excessive warnings against stress and anxiety and any activity that could set off another attack.

"Only that you needed to get out more. True?"

"Well, she didn't mean in the middle of the night. And she didn't mean you had to invite me to your party."

"No, I improvised. Give me a little credit for coming up with my own ideas. Where I come from when somebody has a party, it's only right to invite the neighbors, or they might complain about the noise."

"Where *do* you come from?" she asked, getting up to make coffee. She didn't ask if he wanted any. She hoped he did, because to her surprise she didn't want him to leave right away. She had no idea if he was ready to leave or if he was still enjoying this, this…interlude. She didn't even know why she was enjoying it so much. She just was. She barely knew the man, but she wanted to know him better. She felt at ease in his company, a real rarity.

It felt good to share food and conversation with him. And she wasn't ready for the evening to be over. She, the ultimate loner, had to admit to herself that she craved company tonight. And not just any company. He was special. He was different from anyone she'd ever known. He teased her. He treated her like she was normal. That was a first. She'd always been different. How different he didn't really need to know.

First, she was used to doing everything alone and she liked it that way. She worked alone. Ate alone. Slept alone. She didn't need anybody around. In fact, she'd always liked being alone.

Until now. What had gotten into her? It had started with spring this year and a longing for something she couldn't identify. She was constantly staring out the window, being startled when spoken to, daydreaming. No wonder she was behind in her work. Then she came here and met Max and it further discombobulated her life and her routine. And there was the sleepwalking, a sign all was not normal in her psyche. But so far no attacks. Her inhaler was in the bottom drawer. She prayed it would remain there.

She measured the water and the coffee and waited for his answer. He owed her that. Some kernels of knowledge about himself. After all, he knew two of her dirty little secrets. One, she didn't know how to swim, and two, she was asthmatic. So what was his background? What made him become a divorce lawyer?

"I'm from nowhere and everywhere," he said at last,

tilting his chair back from the table and looking out the window toward her aunt's rose garden. "We moved around a lot, my mom and dad and I." He glanced up at her as she set a cup of coffee in front of him. "I know what you're thinking.

"That I'm a divorce lawyer, because I'm a child of divorce. Not so. My parents should have gotten divorced, they were at each other's throats constantly, bickering, fighting, but they never did it. God knows why. Maybe they were too poor. Or they did it for me. I'd like to think it was for my sake, but I doubt it. They barely noticed I existed. They probably wished I didn't."

She gasped in horror.

"Believe me, I would have been better off without the arguments, without the strife, without the sacrifice on my behalf. I kept wanting to tell them, 'leave, take off, one of you, get rid of each other, this is no way to live.' But I never said anything, and they never did anything. They stayed married. They continued to fight. About everything. About nothing. Believe me, it was enough to make anyone believe in divorce."

"So that's why you became a divorce lawyer," she said, taking the chair across from him, "to spare others the pain of your unhappy home life."

He laughed mirthlessly. "Yeah, that's me, I'm only in it to help people out." He shook his head. "No, sorry. I have to admit, I'm in it for the money. I won't lie to you. Sure, I help people out of difficult situations, but divorce pays well, especially when you're talking large settlements. Money, along with love and affection was in short supply when I was growing up. The reason we moved around so much? The rent was due. We'd pack our suitcases and leave in the middle of the night and leave no forwarding address. If it left me with anything it was a desire to make money, to have a place to live that nobody could throw me out of."

"And to avoid marriage."

He nodded. "That, too."

Sarah couldn't imagine a life on the run like that. It certainly explained a lot about him.

"Not like your childhood, then?" he asked.

"Just the opposite." She stirred cream into her coffee. "I was coddled, spoiled, doted on, treated like an invalid. You talked to my mother, maybe you got a sense? No, well, she's the ultimate in overprotectiveness. I'm surprised she didn't call the police that night you answered the phone. They don't want me here. They never wanted me to move out of their house when I did, even though I only moved three miles away in the city."

"I didn't explain myself to your mom very well," he admitted. "I didn't mean to set off any alarms."

"She'll get over it. My parents have to realize I'm a woman now. That I have a job, I'm responsible, I'm even learning to swim, and that I don't have to call them every night to tell them I'm okay."

"Sounds like you've got your work cut out for you." He reached across the table and took her hand in his.

Such a small gesture. Such a little thing. He didn't mean anything by it. Just a token of support. But just the touch of his warm, strong fingers and her stomach was doing flip-flops, her heart hammering in her chest.

He turned her hand over in his and studied the lines in her palm.

She held her breath, waiting.

"Long and clear life line here," he said, moving his thumb across her palm. Her skin was hot, shivers ran up her spine. "And this." He held her hand up. "See this wavy line above the head line? You know what that is?"

She shook her head. Unable to speak. Good thing she was sitting down, her knees were so weak, she would have collapsed.

He answered his own question. "It's your heart line. And it's very long and deep. Indicating strong and warm feelings. What it means is you've got deep love to give, that will last a long time. You're either in love now or you will be soon. Make sense?"

She cleared her throat. "Not really. How...how do you know all this?"

"An old gypsy told me her secrets. No, I read a book on it once. Actually what I told you is all I know. That's it. Enough to get by. But so far, I've never been wrong."

She drew her hand away and changed the subject.

"I guess most divorce lawyers have been through their own divorces," she said.

"That's right. But not me. I have no intention of getting married. Why put myself through the agony? I've seen it first hand and I don't want any part of it. What about you? Any serious boyfriends?"

"Me?" How had the subject come back to her so fast? "No. And I'm not looking."

"That's when they turn up, when you're not looking. Are you sure there are no men in your life? I can't believe that. Not with your heart line."

"I didn't say no men. There is a man in my life. His name is Secundino Robles. Maybe you've heard of him?"

Max shook his head.

"No? The family is well-known around here. I'm afraid Secundino has spoiled me for anyone else. No one can compare to him. He's six foot three, a blue-eyed native Californio, born in Santa Cruz. A horseman, the best rider in this whole county, a hunter, a miner who struck it rich and a rancher who owned all the land from here to the Bay." She noted the puzzled expression on his face and continued with her tongue-in-cheek and a half smile on her face. "Yes, I'm afraid I wasn't the only woman in his life." She sighed. "But he was the one true love of my life."

"Was?"

"He's dead now."

"I'm sorry," he said. "When did he die?"

"Um, 1890."

Chapter Six

"Did you say 1890?" His jaw dropped. "Don't you think you've had enough time to get over him?"

"Easier said than done," she said with a sigh. "If you'd known him, you'd understand."

"Did you?"

"I think so. At least as well as anyone in this century. I wrote my dissertation on the early Spanish settlers so I've studied his life pretty intensely."

"So you're a real romantic at heart. I knew it. Your palm doesn't lie."

"You could say that. Or you could say I just don't want to face reality, which is what my parents say, my aunt says it, as well as my boss Trudy. Trudy's interested in history, but she's happily married to a great guy and has a life outside the office. She wants to find me someone, but how can anyone compare with Secundino, in his satin jacket, velvet breeches and knee high buckskin boots? Even his horse had silver studded tack." She gazed dreamily off in the distance, as if she listened carefully she'd be able to hear the hoofbeats as Don Secundino galloped across his land toward the foothills.

Sarah didn't know if Max believed her or not. She was half serious about being in love with the past, and especially those swashbuckling heroes from out of history. She didn't blame Max if he thought she was a complete nutcase, but she'd held his interest in any case. He was still there, sitting across the table from her, drinking coffee, his gaze fixed on her, and making no move to go. It was fun to tell stories of the past to someone who'd never heard them. He was a good listener.

"I never would have survived during those days," Max said. "I don't ride or shoot and I've never worn a satin jacket."

"But in other ways you would have fit in perfectly. You have a lot in common with the rancheros. Take your party yesterday. They would have loved it. Like you, they were incredibly hospitable. They were always throwing a feast, a fandango or a barbecue. Guests would party from dusk to sunup. Don't tell me you wouldn't have enjoyed it?"

"I've never turned down a good fandango whatever that is. What about you?"

"I'm not sure if I'd fit in or not. At these parties, the women got together to sew and talk. Of course everyone danced all night and partied till dawn. But I'm not much of a sewer or dancer."

"You're a good talker, though," he said.

She blushed. "I'm talking too much, aren't I? I don't know what's gotten into me. It's your fault for acting so interested."

"It's not an act," he assured her.

She looked across the table at Max in his dark, form-fitting black T-shirt and tried not to stare at the muscles in his upper arms and the abs she knew were there just under the fabric. She was trying to picture him in a wide-brimmed cowboy hat and a satin shirt, but she couldn't. He was macho enough to fit the picture of a ranchero just the way he was. All the more reason that he was out of her league. Way, way out. So she had to stop dreaming. That way she'd never get hurt, dumped or depressed. The best thing for her was to stay away from macho men who lived next door.

If she ever did find someone to share her life, it would be someone as bookish and studious as she was. She could never be interested in someone who helped people get divorced. She'd been brought up to believe that divorce was wrong. That people should take their vows seriously. She could understand why he felt the need to make money after his childhood, but surely there was a more savory profession.

No, she was content to fall in love with someone

from the past who she'd never really know. Men in the present, the ones at the historical society meetings who had so much in common with her, just didn't appeal to her. Sure, they were alive, but just barely.

"There's the question of making a living," Max said. "I might fit into the social life, but what about supporting myself. I don't suppose there were any divorces in those days."

"Actually yes. And women sometimes got big settlements. Like half a ranch. So maybe you would have found a niche for yourself. On the other hand, most rancheros took the law into their own hands to protect themselves. And when a man saw something he wanted, like a woman or a parcel of land, he staked a claim and just grabbed it."

Max leaned forward, his elbows propped on the table, his eyebrows drawn together. "Are you telling me you would have liked living then, without law or order?"

She shook her head. "I never would have survived. The men were tough, but the women were even tougher. As well as cooking and sewing, and giving birth every year, they rode herd with the men. Then there were the raids, the Americans fighting the Mexicans. California was a crazy place. I'm a wimp at heart. I think it's better I'm where I am, square in the twenty-first century, with a car and a job and no wild bears at the door."

"No Secundino, either," Max said with a grin.

She gave a dramatic sigh and a little smile. "That's

right. But I've come to terms with that. I know I can't have everything," she said. "If I can't have Secundino, I won't have anybody." In fact, she'd been reconciled to having no man in her life. No marriage, no kids and no divorce. Nothing to cry over.

Max stood and stretched, giving her a glimpse of a washboard stomach. She tore her eyes away. Standing there, full of sizzling male presence, he made the kitchen shrink to child-size. Her aunt had custom counters made for her five-foot-two petite self and cabinets that were eye-high just for her. The room always looked small, but tonight with him in it, it looked like it was meant for children. Certainly not for six-foot-something macho men.

He glanced at the calendar on the wall. "Your aunt certainly has a full social schedule," he said. "I admire her for being so active at her age."

"So do I," Sarah said, standing and looking at the calendar. "Oh my gosh, the opera. I almost forgot. She left me her tickets, box seats for Friday night. I was supposed to give them away or use them. But I…would you like to go? I'm sure she'd want you to have them. You could invite one of your clients or give them to some couple who are breaking up, because the opera, I think it's something by Strauss, might be just what they need to bring them back together."

Max shook his head. "You are naive, aren't you? If only it was that simple. Strauss made happy music, but I doubt even he could bring divorcing couples together."

"And if they got back together, you'd be out of a job, right?"

"I hope you don't believe I want to see couples split up," he said, his jaw clenched. He turned to leave. "Good night. Thanks for the history lesson."

"Thanks for the dinner," she said, standing and suddenly ill at ease. She shouldn't have said anything about his job. She hadn't meant to malign his profession or give him a history lesson. She just blurted out what she was feeling. Up until then, he seemed to be having a good time, but maybe he was just doing his duty. Just keeping her company as Aunt Mary had requested. "Don't feel you have to stay up on my account. I'm going to lock the doors and sleep downstairs. I'm sure I won't walk tonight."

"If you do, I'll know what to do," he said. He gave her a long, steady look, then his gaze dropped to her lips and she knew exactly what he meant. A kiss. Would he kiss her again? Would she mind? Mind? She wanted him to kiss her. She wanted to be wide awake this time. She wanted to feel his lips on hers. But he didn't kiss her. A few minutes later he was gone. She was alone. And she didn't want to be.

Standing there in the kitchen, she wondered if the first kiss was real or not. She rubbed her lips with the back of her hand. Then she stared at her palm looking at the lines. The life line and the heart line. Was he serious? Did he know anything about palmistry or was he making it all up? She could still feel his thumb brushing her sensitive palm. She could hear his words, *love to give, in love now or will be soon.*

It didn't mean anything. He didn't know what he was talking about. It was a parlor trick, nothing more. But it worked. He had her believing for a few minutes. Only because she wanted to believe. She really wished she hadn't opened her mouth and said what she'd said. What could she do to make it up to him? Insist he take the opera tickets? Yes, that's what she'd do.

That night she stretched a thread across the guest room where she slept and in the morning it was there where she'd tied it to the doorknob. She breathed a sigh of relief. It meant she'd slept peacefully and dreamlessly through the night. Nobody called. She had no attacks of any kind. She was surprised her parents didn't call to find out if she'd drowned. Hopefully they'd gotten the message.

That morning nobody ran a chain saw. Birds twittered outside the open window. The scent of roses and jasmine and grass wafted in. It was a beautiful day.

Sarah tied her hair back from her face in a scrunchie, in her usual slapdash manner, then took a second look at herself in the mirror. New freckles on her pale skin, thanks to falling asleep in the hammock yesterday. She thought about all those glamorous women at the party yesterday and she went up to Aunt Mary's spacious master bathroom with the pale peach walls and the ivory stone tiles.

There in the cabinet behind the wall-to-wall mirror,

was a selection of makeup that rivaled any department store cosmetic department. Too bad Sarah didn't know how to apply the stuff. Nevertheless she smeared some beige liquid makeup over her face. At least it covered her freckles. Then she brushed some blush over her cheekbones which she thought made her look a little more healthy. Then the eyes, blue mascara and eyeliner.

She stared at her reflection. Ridiculous. She looked like a painted doll. What was she doing this for at nine o'clock in the morning? Who was she doing it for and most importantly, why? Max was a flirt, a man who took nothing seriously except his job. He had no intention of getting married or getting serious about a woman. And even if he did, that woman would not be her. She was not his type. It would take months, maybe years before she was ready for a relationship. But even then who would marry her when she told them she had to avoid the stress of pregnancy?

She stared at her face in the mirror. She was an idiot. She scrubbed it all off and went back downstairs.

Then she made a cup of tea and took her laptop out on the terrace with her. She deliberately didn't even glance at the house next door. He said he worked at home, so he was probably inside in his office. But she, who usually worked in a windowless office at the historical society, suddenly couldn't bear to stay indoors on a day like this. She craved the sun and the breeze and the smell of the grass.

On the other hand, when she opened her file to the

chapter on the missions of California, she couldn't remember what she was going to say about them that hadn't already been said. Something had happened to her concentration. Something had disrupted her work ethic.

In this lush garden, under the leafy trellis, with the sun slanting through the trees, she replayed the scenes of the last two days over and over.

When she got tired of that, she gave up on her idea of pretending the man next door wasn't of interest to her and got up and went to the fence between her house and Max's. She leaned over to see if anything was happening, but all was calm, including the surface of the pool which was smooth as glass. She admired the expertly landscaped garden with the huge hydrangea bushes flanking the walkway and the stately eucalyptus trees at the back with their white, peeling bark. She hadn't been able to appreciate it the day of the party when it was crowded with guests or during her swimming lesson when she was full of anxiety. What different lives they led. He liked bunches of people around. She liked solitude. He was fearless, she would like to be, but probably never would be. His parents argued, hers were in agreement on everything. Especially on how to treat their only child.

She glanced up at his house, hoping he wasn't watching from a window, thinking how desperate for company she must seem to be, leaning over and gawking like a tourist or a lovesick neighbor. Of course if he did see her there, and he came out to see her, she'd just say she was watering the flowers. Fortunately the watering can was right between the rosebushes. It didn't have any water in it, but there was time for that.

She heard a car pull up in his driveway and the car door slam shut. She was so rattled she forgot what her excuse was for hanging over his fence, and jumped back. Oh, yes, the watering can. She picked it up and stood there, holding her breath, waiting and watching and practicing what she was going to say. Something about the weather or her swim lesson.

The next thing she heard was someone pounding on Max's front door.

"Max, open up. It's me, Lila," came a high voice.

More pounding, more shouting. "Where are you? I know you're home." The woman sounded desperate.

Then she came around the back of the house. She was tall with flaming-red hair. Her skin was pale, but she had no freckles, or if she did, they were expertly covered with makeup, and she was stunningly attractive in short white shorts, smooth, tanned long legs, a tight, low-cut T-shirt and a big straw bag over one arm.

"Have you seen him?" she asked Sarah.

"Max?"

"No, Ralph Nader," she snapped. "Of course Max. I have to see him. Now. Immediately."

"No, I haven't seen him. Are you sure he's not home?"

"Unless he's hiding from me. But why would he do

that? I'm one of his best clients. Divorce number four coming up. What about you?" the woman asked, taking her sunglasses off to observe Sarah more closely. "Are you a client or just a neighbor?"

"Me? Neither really. I don't live here normally. I'm just house-sitting and I've never been married."

"Well, if you ever do take the plunge, I can recommend Max. As a lawyer, of course. Aside from that, he's a heartbreaker. Ask anyone. Love them and leave them, that's his motto. I guess it's no big surprise. Anyone who's seen the ins and outs of divorce court, naturally they'd be gun-shy. He's got protective armor that even the best can't penetrate. I know. Not that I've tried to pierce it. But I've heard all about it.

"I don't know a woman who hasn't fallen for him. Especially his clients. They're hurt. They're vulnerable. He makes them feel better. He doesn't lead them on, I'll say that for him, he's just being nice, but they don't get the message. Even though he makes it clear he never dates his clients. That's his Golden Rule. And Rule Two, he doesn't get serious about anyone he dates, no matter how attractive they are. When they want to know why, the answer is always the same. If there were fewer marriages, there'd be fewer divorces. He doesn't want to be a statistic. He wouldn't put anyone through the hell of divorce. Especially himself."

Chapter Seven

Sarah stared at the woman in disbelief. She couldn't imagine telling a stranger what this woman was telling her. She apparently needed no encouragement, in fact she hardly noticed Sarah was there. Her mouth never stopped moving. The message she was sending was even more depressing than the messenger. Though it was no surprise to hear he had no interest in marriage. Max had made that very clear.

"But like I said," the woman continued, "if you're the one getting a divorce, and I hope you're not, he's the best. Where would I be without him? I'd be penniless. My ex-husbands didn't know what hit them. You know what he's even better at than settlements?"

Sarah blinked. "Well, no." The woman certainly

went on and on. She wondered how Max would feel to hear her giving this run down on his methods and his rules of behavior.

"Prenups. They're airtight. If you ever get married… You want my advice? Don't fall in love with your husband. Not that I ever made that mistake. It would have made everything so messy."

"I'll keep that in mind."

"I'm Lila, by the way," she said and looked at her watch. "Where could he have gone? He's not an early riser."

Sarah shrugged. She was fairly curious herself. "Have you tried his cell phone?"

Lila nodded. "No answer. I left a message. I think I'll wait around." Lila sat down in a deck chair, stretched her long legs out in front of her, pulled a pack of cigarettes out of her purse and lit one.

Sarah waved the smoke away and stared at the woman. She was so sure of herself, so gorgeous, so rich. She had everything, including the best divorce lawyer money could buy. Everything but love. Why couldn't she find happiness with one man? So this was the kind of person Max dealt with every day. How could he stand it? Even for all the money in the world, she could never put up with that kind of cynicism.

"What went wrong?" Sarah asked, curious in spite of herself, fully expecting the woman to tell her it was none of her business.

Instead she raised her eyebrows in surprise. Maybe she'd forgotten Sarah was still there.

"Wrong? With my last marriage?" She didn't seem surprised or offended at the question. "The usual. He cheated on me."

"That's awful." What a blow that must be, to be betrayed by the one person you thought you could trust.

"Yes, it is."

Sarah backed away from the fence. She'd heard enough. She'd heard too much. It was all so tawdry. "Good luck," she said, for want of anything better.

Lila waved her hand and Sarah went back to her computer. But her mind wasn't on her work. She kept glancing toward the fence, still smelling the faint cigarette smoke that wafted toward her. Wishing Max would come back and do something about his client. Tell her to shape up. Tell her to face up to her own mistakes. To stop being greedy.

When he did, it was even harder to concentrate as they had their consultation, if you could call it that, right across the fence from her.

She didn't know if Max saw her, because he didn't look in her direction, but she saw him and heard everything he said to Lila.

The first thing she saw was Lila throwing herself into Max's arms. Sarah felt a powerful twinge of pain as if she'd been struck by an arrow between her shoulder blades. It couldn't be jealousy. She had no reason to be jealous. Max wasn't anything to her, not even a real neighbor.

The pain increased as Max patted Lila on the back and muttered, "Everything's going to be all right."

Then he asked, just as Sarah had, "What happened?"

Lila burst into tears and Sarah couldn't make out what she was saying until Max held the woman at arm's length and said very loudly, "What?"

"Okay I cheated on him. What was I supposed to do, sit home at night crying into my pillow while he was out with other women?"

"You were not supposed to give him any reason to distrust you. God, Lila, you've been through this before. You knew the rules. Besides, Norm's a friend of mine. You met him through me. You can't possibly expect me…"

"But I do expect you to represent me."

"Not this time."

Lila threw a flowerpot at Max. Sarah jumped up and stifled a scream. Max ducked and the pot hit the side of the house.

Since the pot hadn't struck Max, Lila tried hurling insults. "Pig, rat, scumbag. I'll never trust you again. And I'll never recommend you to any of my friends. Men. You're all the same." A few minutes later she'd stalked out of the yard. Sarah heard the squeal of her tires in the driveway and then it was quiet again.

Sarah didn't move. If she held perfectly still, maybe

Max wouldn't notice she was there. He'd go into his house and then she'd sneak back into hers.

But a moment later, he called to her. "Did you hear that?"

"I'm afraid so," she said. She got up and walked over to his fence. He looked uncustomarily glum. "So that's what a divorce lawyer does to earn his money."

"Nobody ever said it would be easy."

"What does a lawyer do when he knows both partners in the lawsuit?"

"He steps back and lets somebody else handle it. I feel bad for Norm. But I warned him. I told him she was trouble. But he was head over heels." Max shook his head. Worry lines creased his forehead. "I just went to see him. He looks awful. Can't sleep. Can't eat. He says he loved her."

"You don't believe him?"

"I believe he thought he loved her," he said flatly.

"If you had a different job…"

"If I had a different job, I wouldn't have this nice house." He glanced behind him at the trees and shrubs surrounding his sparkling pool. "And what would I do on Sundays, play golf? Boring. That's not me. Sure, there are episodes like this from time to time, hysterical women, angry men, but I can't let it bother me. What bothers me is when my clients don't take my advice. They don't get a prenup or they don't wait until the divorce papers are signed before they're back out there looking for the next husband or wife. They can't stand to be alone. And whatever I did for a living, I still wouldn't believe in love. I mean, what's the point?"

Sarah didn't have an answer for that one. What was the point of falling in love? She'd never done it, so she couldn't speak from experience. For all she knew he was right. It didn't exist except in song and story.

"Did he really cheat on her?" she asked.

"He says he didn't. Until she cheated on him."

"That's awful."

"Now maybe you understand why I don't get married."

"Not everyone's like them," she said. But she did understand. How could she not? She'd just had it all spelled out for her. Who could blame him? First his parents didn't get along, didn't provide an example of a happy marriage, then all his clients. If they were all like Lila, no wonder.

He gave her a long look. He didn't say anything for a few minutes. She felt the tension rise between them. What was he thinking? Was he depressed because of Lila and her husband getting a divorce? Depressed because they hadn't followed his advice? Depressed at the state of matrimony in general?

Finally he spoke. "You know, you're one of the only women I know who hasn't been married or divorced?"

"Really? I'm not sure if that's something to be proud of or not."

"Of course it is. It shows a strength of character. It shows an independent spirit, an ability to stand on your own. Earn your own living, enjoy your own company. You're not even out looking. Hanging out in bars or reading the personals. Or are you?"

She laughed. "No. But I'm not sure I deserve all those things you said about me. Sometimes my own company bores me. Sometimes I wish…nothing."

"You see? You've got what it takes. You have a life. Best of all, you're not angry or bitter. In my experience, it's all too common these days."

Sarah blushed. Although she wasn't sure it was that much of a compliment, considering where he was coming from. If his idea of a typical woman was one like Lila, then yes, she was a rare bird. To be realistic, it wasn't as if she'd turned down a dozen men. It was easy to be single and independent when you didn't have a choice.

"By the way," she said, trying to sound offhand. "Would you like those tickets to the opera on Friday?"

"I'd like one of them."

"You'd go alone?"

"I'd go with you. Isn't that what your aunt would want?"

"I suppose she would. All right." Sarah felt pleased and apprehensive. This wasn't a date. There was no need to be nervous. It was just the opera. But what would she wear?

"Go get your bathing suit," Max said, as if he wasn't worried at all. Why should he be? He'd simply put on a suit that night and enjoy the evening for what it was.

A chance to hear some good music from the best seats in the house. "Time for our next lesson."

Sarah hesitated. Would he think less of her if she quit her swimming lessons? Yes, he would. Was she going to concentrate on the lesson with the water and the sun and her teacher's half naked body with his suntanned skin and well-defined muscles so close to her? Maybe this time he wouldn't have to hold her so tightly. Maybe he'd stand on one side of the shallow end and she'd swim to him. If she could swim at all.

She sighed. "Okay."

Max watched her go, his arms crossed and on the top of the fence, his brow furrowed, his chin resting on his hands. The vision of Lila's face contorted in anger wouldn't leave him alone. Then he thought about poor Norm, who'd fallen for her, despite all advice to the contrary.

Max had to ask himself what he was doing, representing people who couldn't manage their own lives. Was he inadvertently contributing to their problems by making it easy to get divorced and remarried? Because he was good at what he did, his clients only had to throw money at him and all their problems were solved. All except for the emptiness in their lives between marriages. Emptiness that they tried to fill by turning to someone else, over and over again. He rubbed his aching head. This wasn't the first time he was disgusted by a client's issues, but it was the first time he was disgusted with himself for his part in it.

He turned his head and looked at the house next

door. Now there was a different kind of woman. He'd deliberately wangled that invitation to the opera. Not only did he want to hear the music, but he wanted to see what Sarah would look like dressed up.

What was it about this skinny, studious woman that had him so interested? So interested that he'd dreamed about her last night. He would never tell her because it meant nothing. Besides it would only embarrass her. She would blush and look away. It was the contrast, that was it. She was so different from the Lilas of this world.

He smiled to himself at the recollection of his dream. It was the craziest thing. He'd been wearing a satin jacket and riding hell-bent for leather across the golden hills of California. Sarah had been waiting for him behind a curtain in an adobe house, wearing that nightgown he'd seen her in the first night, her long hair cascading over one shoulder. It was her. He was sure it was her.

It was the middle of the night. He'd paused in front of the house and she'd leaped out of the second-story window onto his horse and they'd galloped off into the night. Sitting behind her in the saddle, he held her tightly, as her hair teased his senses, her soft curls blew across his face, the fragrance tantalizing his nose. He was sure she could feel the swell of his physical response as they sat pressed together, with the horse rocking beneath them.

Of course he knew what prompted the dream. It was all that talk about the early days of California's history.

He'd never known much about it, but it was obvious how much she was caught up in it and she'd made it so interesting. He was tempted to tell her about the dream, because she'd appreciate the historical aspects of it. But he wasn't going to. The dream changed nothing, only increased his desire to know her better.

Sure, he'd kissed her that night and he'd dreamed about her, but she didn't know about either incident, and she wasn't going to know. She was the perfect person to lighten up his summer. She was the complete opposite of his clients, especially Lila. He shuddered at the thought of having anything to do with that woman. Sarah wouldn't take anything that happened between them this summer seriously. She wasn't looking for a long-term relationship. Hell, she wasn't looking for anything at all, except to further her career by delving deeper into California's history. The only thing she was serious about was her work. Just like he was. He had the feeling that her work was more satisfying than his. Dangerous thoughts for a man who depended on his income for a lifestyle he intended to hang onto. After five years of divorce law he'd have to start at ground zero if he wanted to do anything else.

Back in her house, Sarah had changed into her swimsuit. She told herself this was an opportunity she couldn't pass up. A chance to learn to swim, a chance to be like the other normal women who bantered with men and put the books aside for a while in the summer. Then there was the opera. Instead of sitting by herself or with a colleague, she'd be sitting next to a really good-looking man who appeared to be interested in her. And not just her mind, her body, too.

Sure, it was a little late for this transformation. She should have started earlier, like in high school the way the other girls did, and gotten it out of her system, but that's the way life was. If her mother hadn't told her not to swim the other day, she wouldn't be so determined to learn. This was better, more convenient and cheaper than going to the YWCA in town. That was all it was. A matter of practicality. It wasn't because of Max.

She had to admit that if she was her usual sensible self, she'd stay away from him. She would have insisted he take both tickets to the opera. He was definitely the sexiest man she'd ever met. And that scared her. She was bewitched by his silver-gray eyes, his arms that wrapped around her and carried her up the stairs. Just standing on the other side of the fence from him made her knees weak and her head spin. Of course she hadn't met all that many sexy men, so maybe she was exaggerating.

His appeal wasn't all physical. He was warm and kind and fun to be around. He confided in her. Told her about his job and his family. She felt like she really knew him. When in reality she barely knew him.

The best thing? He seemed interested in history. How rare was that! In her experience almost unknown. Oh, people pretended to be interested, but she saw the vacant looks, the stifled yawns and the excuses they found to leave the room or hang up the phone. Even her own parents got tired of hearing about California's history.

Max had a winning personality and good looks which were combined into one very attractive package that was hard to resist. As if she'd tried to resist. All she had to do to keep herself from falling under his spell was to remember who she was and who he was.

Yes, he was the man next door. But that was just for a week. He was a divorce attorney, so cynical no woman had ever penetrated his heart. She imagined many had tried. He was that appealing. It was a warning to her that however much she liked him, he could never be more than a friend to her. Which was fine. That was all she wanted. All she expected.

Because she was who she was. She'd made that perfectly clear to him. As if he hadn't seen it for himself. She'd sleepwalked, almost drowned, and went on and on with her tales of California's history. He'd actually encouraged her to tell them to him.

As she was about to walk out the back door, towel in hand, the phone rang. She hesitated. If it was her mother, she didn't want to talk to her. She didn't want to hear any more dire warnings about her asthma. She stood there and let the answering machine pick up. It was Trudy, her boss. She picked up the phone.

"Sarah, I'm sorry to bother you on Sunday."

"Trudy, you sound awful. What's wrong?"

"I…I'm feeling terrible. I don't know, the flu or

something. What I'm wondering is if you could do my elementary school tour at the old general store for me tomorrow? I wouldn't ask because I know you're taking the week off."

"No, no, I'm not on vacation. Not at all. I'm working, I'm writing my paper."

"Oh, that's right, I forgot. This bug I've got has affected my memory."

"Of course I'll do it for you. Where and what time?"

Sarah jotted down the information on a scratch pad. Fortunately the general store in Woodside was actually closer to Sarah's aunt's house than it was to Trudy in the city.

"I'll e-mail you the information," Trudy said. "All you have to do is show up. The costume is in the closet. The teachers will be there with the kids so you ought to have no problem with discipline. I appreciate this, Sarah. I owe you one."

"Don't be silly. I'm glad to do it. Do you think you ought to see a doctor?"

Trudy sniffled. It sounded like she was crying. "No, I'll be all right. I just need...I have to go now."

"Take care of yourself."

Sarah frowned. It wasn't like Trudy to fall apart like that. She hoped it was nothing serious.

"Sorry, I'm late," Sarah said, walking through the gate to the pool. Max was fishing leaves out of the pool with a long pole and a screen at one end. He stopped and gave her a long, slow, appraising look.

Why? He'd seen her in her suit before. She wasn't endowed with gorgeous curves like the other women at his party. She felt her whole body flush with awareness.

"What is it?" she asked, flustered. "Did I get my suit on backwards?"

"Now that would be something to see," he muttered. "No, I think you're getting a little sunburned." He set the pole down, walked over and ran one hand over her shoulder. "Here," he said, then ran the other hand on the curve of her cheek. "And here."

Wherever his hand touched, her skin burned. And that had nothing to do with the sun. It was him. Maybe she was wrong. She couldn't handle swimming lessons with a man like Max. Maybe she should head for the YWCA right away before it was too late and she was in big trouble. But she was trapped by the look in his silver-gray eyes and she knew she wasn't going anywhere. Not anytime soon. Not as long as he treated her like she was a desirable woman.

"I…I put lotion on this time," she stammered. "So I don't think I'll burn."

Burn? She was about to burst into flames from just his touch. She had to get away so she headed for the steps in the shallow end. He jumped in at the other end and swam to her in easy strokes.

"Will I ever be able to swim like that?" she asked when he surfaced next to her.

"Of course. Guaranteed. Or your money back. If you stay long enough that is."

"I only have a week."

"No reason why you can't drive down here for a lesson from time to time when the week is up, is there? I don't think your aunt would mind."

"I hadn't thought of it."

"Think about it."

Sarah couldn't think of anything once they started the so-called lesson. His hands were everywhere, under her arms, around her waist, holding her head up. The water was warm and smooth. She put her head under and didn't swallow any water. She smiled and laughed at the faces he made underwater. She felt silly and giddy, like a little kid in the water for the first time.

She continued to feel giddy and silly until he put his hands on her shoulders and stood looking at her, the water dripping down across the fine hairs on his muscular chest. "You're amazing," he said. "The best student I've ever had."

No more a little kid. Now he made her feel like she was a woman. A woman who was in danger of falling for her swimming instructor. A woman who had no defenses against such blatant masculine charm. The words of Lila echoed in her brain once again and she knew she was not in danger of drowning. She was in more danger of losing her head over a man she couldn't have. She felt light-headed, caught in a web that she couldn't get out of.

"Really," she said.

He grinned at her. He leaned forward and kissed her

lightly on the mouth. Her knees shook, her hands trembled. He tightened his hold on her shoulders. But it was over as fast as it had begun.

What could she do? Kiss him back? Run away? Pretend it never happened? Now how would she do that? One option was to quit right now and take her chances on drowning. She could be rescued from drowning, but from losing her head over a man? What if she was falling in love? Then what? She'd been warned. He was a man who'd successfully escaped all the other women who were falling all over him. Who could rescue her from him?

Chapter Eight

She took a deep breath and forced herself to think rationally. When she got herself under control, she said nothing about the kiss. Instead she focused on what he'd said. "Wait a minute. I'm the only student you've ever had, right?"

"Well, yes, If you want to get technical about it. The secret to your success is that you've relaxed," he told her. "You were nervous the first time."

"I'm still nervous," she said. Her stomach was full of butterflies going crazy. But it wasn't the swimming that made her nervous. It was him. "I feel like I'm having a delayed adolescence. I spent all my other summers indoors. I'd hear the other kids outside, but I could never go out for fear I'd have an asthma attack."

"Poor Sarah," he said, brushing her cheekbone with the pad of his thumb.

Oh, no, this was a mistake. This kind of touch, the kind that sent her blood pressure soaring, was not part of the deal. She bit her lip. "But I'm making up for lost time. I'm having a good time," she said earnestly. There, that ought to set the tone back to normal.

But it didn't. He said, "So am I." His smile dazzled her more than the summer sun. She found herself smiling back. They stood there like that as the water lapped against her bare skin and the sun shone on her shoulders, just smiling like idiots. This time she wasn't surprised when he kissed her. She expected it. She wanted it.

He tasted like sun and summer and all outdoors and all the good times she'd missed. She hadn't been kissed that often, like hardly ever, but this was a different kiss than any she'd ever had and she knew somehow this was a dynamite kiss, one that was ripe with promise. One that left her breathless and wanting more.

What did it promise? Nothing, she told herself sternly. She instructed herself to get real. She turned and waded out of the pool. Maybe that was rude or silly. After all, it was just a kiss. He didn't mean anything by it. But for her, it was something amazing. Something to think about, to dream about.

"Where are you going?" he asked. He sounded puzzled. She didn't turn around.

"Just, uh, to dry off. That was great." She felt the heat

sweep up her face. Maybe he thought she meant the kiss. "I mean the lesson."

"I knew that," he said. This time she could tell he was smiling. "Till tomorrow, then?" he said.

She turned to look at him, still standing waist-deep in the pool, his wet hair standing on end, making him look so endearing she wanted to get back in the pool and kiss him back. Of course her kissing ability was nonexistent and he'd know it as soon as she tried. Let him kiss her if he wanted to, she'd just sit back and enjoy it.

"We'll take up where we left off," he said with a knowing grin.

She wrapped her towel around herself.

"I mean the lesson," he said.

"I knew that," she said. Then she walked to her gate. "Oh, wait. I might not have time for a lesson, because tomorrow I have to give a tour to some school children at a historical site. The old country store in Woodside."

"On the corner of Tripp Road? I've seen that. Always wondered what it was. Can anyone go inside?"

She glanced at him over her shoulder. "If you're in fifth grade and your teacher takes you there."

"That lets me out," he said. "What about if you know the tour leader? Would that help?"

"Well…"

"Maybe I wouldn't fit in."

Sarah smiled at the picture of the six-foot-three-inch, strapping male hunk in the low-ceilinged wooden structure with a roomful of restless schoolchildren as she gave her lecture on life in the 1800s while dressed in the period costume. Would they notice him? How could they not? Would she be distracted? How could she not be? Why would he want to come? It was hardly a Hollywood production.

"It's not that."

"What is it?" he asked. "You've awakened my interest in California's history. Sounds like this is an opportunity for me to actually see something real, something I've always been curious about. It is real, isn't it?"

"The structure's been restored, but it gives a good picture of what life was like in those days for people like loggers and blacksmiths, ordinary people. Of course if you want to come, you can, but I don't think…"

"What time?"

"The tour starts at ten. I thought I'd leave about nine. Give myself time to get into my costume and practice my speech."

"Costume? Speech?" He raised his eyebrows. "It gets better and better."

"We keep it pretty simple, really. Even the fifth-graders have a hard time focusing if we don't. They're used to TV and video games and even though we try to make it interesting, it's an uphill battle to compete with the media. I don't want you to get your hopes up. It's just me and the setting. No special effects. No guns, no horses."

"That's too bad," Max said. "But I'm coming anyway. I'll stay in the background and blend in. I won't say a word. I just wanted to see the place and what you did for a living." She didn't look completely convinced that he sincerely wanted to be part of her audience. She mostly looked puzzled by his enthusiasm.

If she was confused by his behavior, he was even more puzzled. Was it really California's history that interested him? Or was it his neighbor, a most unusual woman? After Sarah went home, he swam a few laps to expend some pent-up energy and to think things over. He wasn't sure what had come over him. Was it the contrast between Lila and Sarah that made Sarah look so innocent and sweet that he had to kiss her twice? He knew one thing, he had no business coming on to her.

She didn't know how to handle it. And neither did he, for that matter. He liked having her for a next-door neighbor, if only for a week. He liked having her for a friend. She was so earnest, so cute without knowing it and so devoted to her subject that her enthusiasm was contagious.

If he wanted to keep her as a friend, and he definitely did, at least for the week, he'd have to make sure there were no more kisses, no matter how softly enticing those lips were. There could be nothing wrong with a trip to a historical site as long as there were mobs of schoolchildren as witnesses. There could be nothing wrong with going to the opera with her. Even if he wanted to kiss her there, he couldn't. Not with all those people around. That was the secret. Avoid situations where they were alone.

Did that mean discontinuing swimming lessons? Forget that. He was already looking forward to the next one. It gave him the perfect excuse to hold her, touch her, get close to her without setting off alarm bells. He knew she was skittish, so he had to be careful. She was so lovely, so natural, so unspoiled. He didn't want to change her. He didn't want her to turn into one of those hardened divorcées he dealt with every day. No chance of that. She was married to her work. And as she said, no one could compete with that swashbuckling hero of hers.

Friends. They would be friends. Nothing more. Nothing less. He had woman friends like Lila whose divorces he'd handled, but when things didn't go their way, and they didn't get the settlements they thought they deserved, their friendship was over. He wasn't surprised to find his clients were greedy, but it was always a disappointment.

With Sarah they could be real friends, as long as he could keep his libido intact. That shouldn't be a problem.

It shouldn't have been a problem, but it was. Sitting next to her in his Porsche on the way to the Woodside Store—he'd insisted on driving though she had planned on taking her car—she looked so fresh and innocent in light summer seersucker cropped pants, a white sweater and sandals he wanted to reach over and put one hand on her thigh. But he didn't. He wanted to take that strand of silky hair that blew across her face and tuck it behind her ear. But he didn't. Instead he offered to listen to her practice her speech.

She seemed a little off balance. She had to keep referring to her notes, which appeared to be out of order.

He wondered if she was nervous about making the speech. He couldn't imagine her not being ready and eager to share her knowledge with schoolchildren, with all the energy she used when talking to him.

When they arrived at the restored wooden structure known as the Woodside Store, she was her calm, confident self again and seemed to enjoy showing Max around the musty-smelling, low-ceilinged building.

"This building was a multiuse structure back in the heyday of lumbering. It was a store, a post office and a dental office. All at one time. A dentist named Dr. Tripp practiced here, so you could have your tooth pulled, buy a bag of flour and, if you were a prospector, buy a pick and a shovel. Then you could pick up your mail from your loved ones back East."

"One-stop shopping," Max commented.

"Exactly. Tripp and his partners in the sawmill business were from Massachusetts. They came to California to make their fortunes. Like so many others, Levi Strauss, Leland Stanford and the others who came to look for gold, they made more money selling goods to the miners than many of the miners made.

"Because of the gold rush, there was a huge demand for building materials in San Francisco, so the entrepreneurs who worked around here like Parkhurst, 'Grizzly' Ryder and Tripp dragged the logs down to the bay and floated them to the city."

"Tripp was quite a multitasker, logging as well as running this store and pulling teeth too," Max said.

"That's right. In the old days, you had to do everything yourself or it didn't get done." She glanced at her watch. "I've got to get my dress on before they come."

If he thought it was hard to keep his hands off her in the car, he was even more tempted to touch her when he saw her in her costume, a figure-hugging cotton dress. It was long with a high neck made of a fabric with little flowers dancing across it that fit tightly across her breasts and waist. He couldn't keep from staring at her small round breasts hugged by tight fabric.

"This dress doesn't fit me. I can't breathe," she said, appearing flushed and nervous from the closet where the costumes were kept. "And I haven't even fastened the buttons."

"I think it looks great on you," he said, stifling a lecherous smile. "Let me." Before she could protest, he stepped behind her and was buttoning the dress from the back, his fingers fumbling as if he was on a first date. He noticed she wasn't wearing a bra. But she had been earlier. He'd definitely noticed that. "How's that?" He asked when he'd finished. He put his hands on her shoulders and turned her around to face him.

"Fine," she said breathlessly. He stepped back and admired the dress, and even more the woman inside the dress. Her hair was hanging in tendrils around her face. Her cheeks were pink and her blue eyes were bright. If this was 1847, and he was a logger come to town to pick up supplies, he would have definitely tried to pick her up, too. So would all the other men in town. He might not even have a chance, competing with all those macho men of yesteryear. But he'd give it a try. He knew that.

"So this is an authentic dress?" he asked, taking the opportunity to observe her from head to toe. After all, it was just in the interest of historical research.

"It's not really old, but it's made to match the pictures we have of the styles of the day. Obviously made for someone a little smaller than me."

"I'd say it fits just right. Did they, uh, did the women wear underwear back then?"

Her already flushed face turned crimson. "Of course. They wore corsets and…and…why do you ask? Oh, I see, because I'm not. Is it that noticeable?" She folded her arms across her breasts.

"No, it's just when I was buttoning your dress I couldn't help noticing there was no…that you weren't wearing anything. But from the front, it's not at all obvious," he lied. With a huge effort, Max kept his eyes on her face. He didn't let his gaze stray below her neck for fear of making her more self-conscious. But the harder he tried to avoid looking at her breasts, the more he wanted to.

"Maybe if I put on the hat it will help." She reached to the top shelf above the cans of beans and bags of sugar and lifted a large, dusty hat down and set it on her head. "Don't laugh," she said, tossing the veil back so she could see him.

"I wasn't," he insisted, biting his tongue. "It looks great on you, really."

Outside a yellow school bus pulled up and thirty schoolchildren, with two teachers and a few parents came noisily bursting into the wooden structure. Max was impressed by the way Sarah handled them. All her nervousness disappeared and she took charge, calming the children, introducing herself, and then launching into her speech. She spoke so naturally and so enthusiastically, she gave the impression she was speaking off-the-cuff. First she explained that the store became most important and popular in 1853 when the stagecoach service arrived. Until then, because of the small population, the store struggled, and often the local residents were on their own when it came to buying supplies.

Dr. Tripp, she said, expanded the store, and operated it until his death in 1909. He was a legendary character because of the many roles he played in frontier life.

As she launched into the storekeeper's biography, Max stepped to the back of the musty, dusty interior lined with shelves and filled with tools and implements as well as supplies. He leaned against the wall and watched with admiration as Sarah became a woman from a different era.

It was her dress and her hat but it was also her voice and her manner. She made history come alive. She was wonderful. He wasn't the only one who admired her.

The students crowded around Sarah, and she answered their questions patiently and with good humor. She seemed genuinely interested in them. No matter how silly or trivial their questions, she answered them all.

"Where's the bathroom?"

"Did they sell candy at the store?"

"Did the kids have to go to school?"

"Did everyone have a horse?"

"How much did stamps cost?"

"Are you married?"

The last one made her blush and look down at her laced-up, period-style boots. Then she gracefully changed the subject.

She launched into stories of some of the colorful characters like Captain John Greer, who explored San Francisco Bay, and Juana Briones, the most famous woman of her time. The kids knew her name, because there was a school named after her, but they didn't know why she was famous.

Then there were tales of the men and women who'd braved a long trip from the East Coast to make new lives for themselves. She told funny stories and sad stories about the owners and the customers of the store.

Then it was over. The class chanted, "Thank you, Miss Jennings," and they filed out of the dusty old general store into the sunlight to picnic on the grounds.

Sarah gave a sigh of relief. Max closed the door after the last child had walked out and carefully lifted her large, ridiculous hat off her hair. His warm fingers grazed the side of her cheek and she felt the color rise in her face. Then he hugged her. She nervously looked out the windows, not sure what the kids would think if they'd seen that, but they were busy opening their brown lunch bags at the picnic tables.

"You did good," he said, his eyes bright, a big smile on his face.

His enthusiasm was contagious. She was pleased with the way it had gone. She was also relieved. She felt like throwing her arms around Max and dancing around the general store, like Juana Briones would have done, but she wasn't anything like the pioneer woman. She was a staid and studious historian.

So instead of dancing, or acting out of character, she took a deep breath and went to change out of her dress. When she was able to breathe normally again, she straightened the shelves and locked the doors behind her. Max was waiting for her just outside the door in the sunshine.

"You were so convincing as a frontier woman," he said, "I could have sworn you came from a different time. You looked the part, you acted the part and the kids loved it."

"Really?" She beamed happily. He made her feel like a Broadway star when all she'd done was to tell the true stories, the same stories that made her love history.

"You know, I've given talks before, but never here and never to little kids. I was nervous. I've seen Trudy give the talk. She's really good and the dress fits her."

"She couldn't be better than you were. You heard the kids' questions. They were really interested. You may have inspired a whole new generation of future historians."

"That would be nice, but even if they just have an appreciation of how hard life was then and how easy it is now, it will be worth it."

"Now what?" he asked. "I see the kids brought their sack lunches, but we didn't. What if we had a picnic down by the bay, down where they floated their logs to San Francisco? In the interest of history, of course. I'm not ready to return to the twenty-first century. Maybe we could eat sourdough bread like the miners did."

Sarah felt exhilarated. She'd done a good job. Even without praise from Max, she knew she had. She didn't want to go home and go back to writing her paper. The idea of a picnic was enticing. "You know there were dairy farms up in the hills. So we could have cheese and eat the way they did."

"And wine. They had wine, didn't they?"

"Definitely. Of course they kept livestock, so we could have a pork or chicken product."

"Wouldn't we have to raise it first?" he asked.

She frowned. "If we want to be authentic."

"I'm kidding. Let's hit the real store and see what they've got. That history lesson has given me an appetite."

"But are you sure you don't have work to do?" she asked. It occurred to her he was spending a lot of time with her. Was he really that interested in history, or… why would he be interested in her, unless he still felt he owed it to her aunt?

She wasn't his type. She'd been duly warned about him and she took Lila's warnings seriously. Not that she cared whether he was a love 'em and leave 'em type of guy. She wasn't looking for love, just a little lightening up of her life. Just a little flirtation. The problem was she didn't know how to flirt. But he did. Maybe that was good enough.

"I have to ask you something," she said as they walked toward his car.

He stopped and looked at her. She thought there was a flicker of alarm in his eyes. Was he afraid she expected something from him? Was he going to tell her how they could only be friends and nothing more? She knew that. She took a deep breath. She had to know. Even if the answer was yes.

"Are you being nice to me because you owe it to my aunt?"

Chapter Nine

"Of course not," he said.

"But she did do some favors for you, didn't she?"

"She signed for my deliveries when I wasn't there, she let the carpet installers in. She has a key to my house. I have one to hers. She did all kinds of favors. What does that have to do with anything?"

"Because if you're only doing this…"

"This hanging out with you, goofing off in my pool, sharing my leftovers, is that what you mean?"

"And coming with me today," she added. "Because if you are," she continued, ignoring his question, "you don't have to. Your obligation is fulfilled."

"You think so?" he said. "I'll have to check with your aunt about that. And since she isn't here, I'm afraid you'll have to continue to put up with my attempts at recompense." He opened the car door for her, got in and started the engine.

"Maybe I should ask *you* something," he said as he pulled out of the parking lot. "Did you offer me a ticket to the opera only because your aunt insisted on being nice to me, or do you really want to go with me?"

"Both," she said without thinking.

"Okay, here are some more questions for you. Are you tired of my interfering with your work? Do you wish I wouldn't come knocking on your door with my leftovers and tagging along with you today? Say it, you won't hurt my feelings. If it does, I'll get over it. It won't be the first time."

"I don't believe you. I don't believe anyone's ever told you to buzz off. Any woman, that is."

He shot her a puzzled look. "Why do you say that? You weren't talking to Lila, were you, because she has a warped vision of me."

"I wouldn't say I was talking to her, but she was sure talking to me."

"About me," he said grimly.

"Well, yes," she admitted. Now she was sorry she'd ever started this conversation. It was getting far too intense. "Don't worry, it was nothing personal." That was a lie. It was all personal. "You know a lot more about me than I do about you."

"You're referring to what I learned while reading your palm, is that it?"

She slanted a glance in his direction, relieved to see he was grinning at her.

"It was a very impressive display of your many talents. I had no idea my whole life could be revealed via my palm."

"Look, Sarah," he said, suddenly serious. "Whatever Lila said about me, I'm not the kind of guy who hangs around when he's not wanted. Is it so hard to realize that I don't need an excuse to spend time with you? Sure, I owe your aunt big time, but that has nothing to do with us."

Sarah blinked. Did he say *us?* Surely there was no *us.* What did it mean?

"Let's pretend you're the neighbor, not your aunt," Max continued. "Let's say I don't owe you anything and vice versa. I like you. I'm having a good time. Are you?" He slanted a glance in her direction.

"Me?" Now he'd turned the conversation and his gaze back to her. She wasn't used to talking about herself. She wasn't used to being looked at the way he looked at her when she was squeezed into that too-tight dress. She wasn't used to being kissed, either. But he must know that. It must be abundantly clear she'd had no experience with men. Especially men like him.

"Yes, you." He reached over and put his hand on her thigh. She felt the warmth of his palm right through the light cotton fabric of her capri pants. She licked her dry lips and tried to catch her breath.

"You're cute and funny. And you're different."

Cute? Funny? She'd been called many things, mostly *smart, interesting,* or *hardworking,* but never cute or funny. "You mean I'm different from your clients? Like Lila? I hope so."

Instead of answering he leaned over and brushed his lips across her cheek. She swallowed hard. She never knew what he was going to do next.

"I'm glad to hear it otherwise I'd feel sorry for you."

He pulled into the parking lot of an upscale grocery store used by Silicon Valley types who lived in this woodsy suburb. They stood in front of the deli case trying to decide what would be appropriate.

"You said pork was all right," Max said. "Because they had livestock. Then how about some pâté laced with port wine?"

She nodded and they also selected a wedge of Brie cheese. They picked up a fresh baguette from the bakery section and a then filled a sack with vine-ripened tomatoes, a basket of strawberries and a pound of white peaches. And a bottle of chilled Pinot Grigio.

"Fortunately I have a Swiss Army knife in my car," he said as they drove toward the Bay, "and a blanket."

"Sounds like this isn't your first impromptu picnic," she said lightly. But she felt a pang of unattractive jealousy hit her. What was wrong with her, why couldn't she just accept him for what he was, a commitment-shy divorce lawyer who, according to him, enjoyed her company, thought she was entertaining and cute.

It was ridiculous, but he made her feel like a different person. He made her feel cute. It even made her act cute. When she wasn't acting jealous, that was. Suddenly she imagined dozens of women picnicking with him on his blanket. Drinking wine and feeding each other strawberries while the juice dribbled down their chins.

"As a matter of fact, it is my first impromptu picnic," he said. "But it may not be the last, if all goes as planned."

"Planned?"

"I plan to sit on the grass, with a bottle of wine, a loaf of bread and thou beside me," he said, sending her a glance that was half teasing, half serious and that made her grip the leather seat tightly with stiff fingers. It was one thing to be nice to her because her aunt asked him to. Or because he was enjoying a break from his work, or because California's history was so fascinating.

But this was out-and-out flirting, and she didn't know quite how to handle it. She realized that one-sided flirting didn't work. Flirting was more fun when both parties took part. She didn't know how to flirt back. And even if she did, should she? Wasn't she just setting herself up for a huge letdown when she left and went back to her real life?

"How many divorce lawyers can quote Khalil Gibran?" she wondered out loud.

"Were you impressed? I hope so. You're not the only one who lives in the past. I always wanted to be a caliph."

"So you could have a harem?"

He shook his head. "I can hardly handle one woman at a time, let alone a harem."

She wished she could think of a reply to that, but she couldn't, so they drove in silence toward the Bay. From time to time she sneaked glances in his direction, admiring his profile, the firm jaw, the wide mouth and his hands on the steering wheel. She could still feel the brush of his lips on her cheek. She remembered the touch of his hands on her back as he fastened her dress this morning. And she wondered how they'd feel on her bare skin if she'd wriggled out of the dress.

What if she'd been one of those real California seductresses with dark flashing eyes and dozens of suitors? If she were, she'd have let the dress pool around her ankles on the floor. Then she'd have turned and offered her bare breasts to the man she loved. He would have covered them with his hands, teased her nipples and buried his face in the hollow between her breasts. What if that had happened today, and they'd been alone in the old store, no schoolchildren on their way? Then what?

Her heart pounded at the possibilities. Even though she knew they were just that. Possibilities and not probabilities.

For the first time in her life, she admitted that was what she wanted, even needed. She wanted his hands on her skin, his mouth on hers, his arms around her, pressing his body to hers. He'd be good at it, she knew

he would. According to Lila, he'd had years of experience with loads of women who he'd eventually
dumped. That's what she needed, a man of experience,
to teach her how it was done.

By the time he turned off and went down a bumpy
road she was breathing hard and staring out the side
window trying to pull herself together. Max drove his
car into a lot next to a marshy area with a wooden
boardwalk and nature signs pointing to the Bay. They
carried their grocery bags and their blanket toward a
grassy knoll overlooking a duck pond as if they'd been
doing it this way for eons. But all the while her pulse
was racing. A picnic, she told herself. Nothing to get
excited about. A picnic in a public place. What could
happen? What did she want to happen?

There were a few children with parents feeding the
ducks, but they moved on after a few minutes, and then
the only sounds were the water lapping against the
shore of the pond and the scrub jays screeching at each
other in the trees overhead.

Instead of cutting the bread, he ripped off a hunk, cut
a piece of cheese and gave them to her. Then he opened
the wine with the corkscrew attachment on his Swiss
Army knife and handed her the bottle. His hand brushed
hers. This time she thought it was deliberate, and she
felt a jolt of awareness. She thought he did, too.

A jug of wine, a loaf of bread and thou beside me…

"No glasses, sorry," he said.

She shrugged and drank the wine straight from the

bottle. The cool, fruity essence slid easily down her throat and left a warm trail. Above their heads was a canopy of silver maples. A few more sips of wine and she felt light-headed and reckless.

She reached for a tomato and bit into it. It was tart and sweet and tasted like it had just been picked in someone's garden. She glanced at him and saw he was watching her.

"What is it? Do I have tomato all over my chin?" She grabbed a napkin and rubbed it across her chin.

"You have 'I'm having a good time' written all over your face. Why don't we do this more often?" he asked.

She laughed. "You can do this every day," she said lightly, "since you claim to work at night. But unfortunately I work during the day. In fact, I should be working now."

"You *were* working. You're allowed a lunch break, I hope."

"Sure," she said. But she thought, a lunch break, yes, but a picnic with wine and a handsome, flirtatious neighbor? She felt like she was in a movie, beautiful scenery, wonderful food and a movie-star-look-alike companion. Where did she fit in to the picture? If this were a movie, she'd be the technical consultant, making sure the historical details were accurate. But the star? The romantic interest? If she spent any more time with him, she'd begin to believe it might be possible.

Max's cell phone rang. He frowned and looked at the number. No one he knew. He switched it off. He didn't want to be reminded of his work, his clients and his other life. He was having too much fun hanging out with Sarah, living her life for a change. He shoved the phone into his back pocket. Maybe he'd lost a new client. Maybe not. Right now he didn't care.

He really wondered why he couldn't do this more often. He could. Then why couldn't she? Just because her aunt was returning at the end of the week didn't mean he couldn't see her again. As friends of course. He had no intention of coming on to her. That one kiss didn't mean anything. Not to him, not to her, either. She wasn't the type for a flirtation or a brief affair. She didn't date and if she did, she would take it seriously. He knew that.

What he should do was forget about her at the end of the week. He knew, or he ought to know, that friendship between men and women was difficult if not impossible. But just a glance in her direction, seeing her hair tossed by the breeze, dark wisps on her cheek, and watching her bite into a ripe strawberry, her lips stained red, he was not ready to say goodbye to her for good.

He drank from the wine bottle and tasted her lips there. It wasn't enough. He wanted more than a taste. He needed more. Maybe it was the sun. Maybe it was the warm air. Maybe it was her. He leaned across the blanket and framed her face in his hands. Her eyes widened. Such huge blue eyes filled with questions. He had no answers, but he had some questions of his own.

What's wrong with a kiss between friends?

Do you really want me to back off?

Can't we just relax, stop worrying, and see where this leads?

Are you having as good a time as I am?

What if we did have a brief fling, would that be so bad?

Yes, was the answer to that last question. Yes, it would. It would be bad for everyone. Her aunt would find out. She'd get excited. She'd want to know why it couldn't last. Mary liked Max, but she liked her niece even better. Mary would blame him for leading Sarah on. He'd feel guilty. It would be awkward living next door to Mary, dodging her, not knowing what to say.

And worst of all? Sarah would realize what a deliciously desirable woman she was and she'd find someone to take his place when they broke it off. She was so attractive, she just didn't know it. One taste was not enough. But sooner or later they would break it off. No two people could be less alike than Sarah and him. She thought what he did for a living was somehow unworthy. She thought he took advantage of people's weaknesses and greed. She could be partly right.

As much as she'd interested him in California's history, he was quite aware that she lived in the past too much. He didn't intend to get married. She didn't plan on it, but he thought she probably would. Why not? She would make some man happy with her lively imagination, her stories of the past, her enthusiasm for the present and her willingness to try new things. Like swimming, flirting and kissing and whatever it led to. She'd make someone a great companion, wife, lover and friend.

Despite all the reasons for backing off, there was that eager wide-eyed look on her face that said yes, yes, yes, and suddenly all his scruples were gone, as well as all the negative thoughts racing around his head. He threw caution to the winds and kissed her again. A kiss, that's all it was.

No sweet, exploratory kiss this time. They only had a week together. Might as well make the most of it. This time he angled his mouth and kissed her so hard and so thoroughly she leaned backward, farther and farther until her head was on the blanket. He fell foreword, bracing his arms on either side of her shoulders.

Then she kissed him back. Sarah, the shy, quiet, introverted historian, brushed her lips against his and then shyly slid her tongue into his mouth. He felt like he was on fire.

"Sarah?" he muttered. As if he wasn't sure it was her.

Her answer was to wrap her arms around his neck, pull him to her and bury her face in the curve of his jaw. He kissed the tender spot below her ear, he trailed kisses along her cheek, until his lips met hers again.

With his body on top of hers, every hard masculine angle pressed into her soft curves, Sarah had never felt so small, so feminine and so desirable. She'd never felt so alive, either, every nerve, every molecule on fire. She wished she could get closer to him, but little twigs and small stones were embedded into her back, right through her shirt. Not that she cared. She was beyond thinking, beyond caring what happened. All she knew was that she'd never felt this way before.

They rolled over. Now she was on top of him. He grinned up at her, his eyes silvery-gray. She felt the heat from his body, his warm breath on her face. So this was what it was all about. This was what she'd been missing all her life. If she'd only known.

She couldn't believe she was doing this. She had never imagined she could be the object of somebody's wild desire. She felt beautiful and sexy. It was all because of him. She was twenty-five years old and she was falling in love. Falling in love? In three days? Impossible. Falling in lust was more like it.

He kissed her again and she kissed him back. Again and again. Faster and harder and more intense with each kiss. She was no longer worried about her technique or lack of it. No longer worried about the future or if there was one. The only thing that worried her was that he might stop. All she cared about was him and the present. About the way his mouth felt on hers, and the way his hand felt reaching under her shirt, caressing the bare skin of her stomach and tracing the outline of her breasts.

She moaned deep in her throat and wondered where that sound came from. It couldn't be her. Not strait-laced, virginal Sarah who'd hardly ever been kissed, let alone ravished on a grassy field by a man she scarcely knew. Her skin burned, her body ached and cried out for more.

She hated the barriers between them. She wanted to rip off her clothes and his, too. She didn't. She wouldn't. She couldn't. But oh, how she wanted to.

It was all so perfect. The smell of fresh grass, the scent of wildflowers and the sun filtering through the leaves. Like a scene out of that movie she'd been fantasizing. Somewhere a woodpecker was high in the oak tree above them hammering away. Just like her heart was hammering against her ribs.

Even louder was the blood pounding in her ears. The voice inside her that repeated urgently, *now, now, now.* Until the sound of voices came from out of nowhere and silenced that voice in her head. Children's voices and their footsteps. Max heard them, too. She wrenched herself away from him, rolled over and lay flat on her back in the grass, one hand over her eyes. He was lying next to her, panting, gasping for breath. So was she.

She sat up, yanked her shirt down and brushed the grass and twigs off her pants. Just in time. They came marching around the bend, at least a dozen little kids, wearing red T-shirts with the name of a nursery school stenciled on the front, stopping at the edge of the pond, their little voices echoing across the water.

These were little children, little impressionable children who would have most certainly been shocked if they'd seen two adults rolling around in the grass, tear-ing at each others' clothes. On the verge of whatever it was they were on the verge of. Sarah shivered at the thought. What would they have done if the group hadn't arrived?

What would her boss have thought? What would her parents have thought? What would Aunt Mary have done if she'd known what a simple neighborly act had led to? Maybe this was what she'd had in mind. Maybe this was what she wanted to happen.

The kids stopped at the pond and threw food to the ducks. In actuality, they hardly bothered to look at the two adults who were sitting or rather sprawling on a blanket, the remains of a picnic lunch tossed to one side and an empty wine bottle on its side.

Sarah sat on the blanket, her chin resting on her knees drawn up in front of her, staring unseeing at the kids and the ducks, and taking deep cleansing breaths as she tried to feel normal again. Not that she really wanted to go back to her normal life.

As for Max, she was afraid to turn and look at him. The last time she looked, he appeared to be comatose.

"Time to go?" she asked, in what she hoped was her ordinary voice.

He didn't answer, he just sat up and stuffed the leftovers into the grocery bag, then silently got to his feet. She didn't know what he was thinking. Was he sorry they'd come here? Was he even sorrier he'd lost his head and made a scene in a public park?

Back in the car, he drove slowly back to town. He

didn't speak. Neither did she. The silence was painful. She racked her brain for something to say. Her mind was blank.

"Sarah," he said at last. "We have to talk."

Chapter Ten

But his cell phone rang before he could say whatever it was he was going to say. All the way home he talked to a client about her divorce. Sarah didn't want to hear about the woman's problems. From what she could hear, Max was all ears, treating her with kid gloves, sympathizing with her position and promising to get her everything she deserved. No wonder he was so good at his job. So good it was depressing.

From the one side of the conversation she heard she gathered that the woman had been dumped and was in the depths of despair. It was disturbing to think of some poor woman struggling to make ends meet just because she had been discarded like yesterday's trash. Lucky for her, she could afford a high-priced lawyer like Max.

But what if she had no money, did Max take on such cases? Did he take them on spec? At the end of the conversation she heard him set up an appointment with the woman for that afternoon at his house. He hung up just as he pulled into his driveway. Sarah wanted to ask him about the case. But of course it was none of her business. He was probably sworn to secrecy because of attorney-client privilege.

In a way she was grateful for the phone call. It meant she didn't have to hear what Max had to say to her. She could only imagine what it would be.

I didn't mean for that to happen.

It was my fault. I shouldn't have kissed you. I shouldn't have suggested a picnic.

You're a very attractive woman, but...

We shouldn't see each other again for obvious reasons.

You were right about your aunt. I was only doing this because she asked me to.

All Sarah wanted was to get out of the car, run inside her house and close the door behind her.

Which was exactly what she did.

When she turned to look back over her shoulder, she saw he was standing in his driveway, watching her go, a strange look on his face. The look could have meant any number of things. What Sarah thought was that it was one of relief. She knew just how he felt because she felt the same.

She went back to her computer and stared at images

of adobe houses and the missions of California, each mission constructed one-day's horseback ride from the other. Many of them still intact, now turned into museums visited by thousands of tourists every year. She'd been to them all, taken pictures of them, steeped herself in the atmosphere, until she knew how it would have felt to have been a Spanish missionary or a Native American pressed into servitude, to work the fields around the mission, to paint the church or to try to run away from an alien culture.

Usually that's all it took to get her fired up. Not today. Even though she knew she had a whole chapter to write by the end of the week for the pamphlet published by the historical society, she couldn't write a word. All she could think about was Max and how he looked bending over her in the dappled sunlight.

If it hadn't been for the children, what would have happened? Surely she would have come to her senses and jumped to her feet and put a stop to it. Or would she? Was she so enamored, so blown away by this man, she would have risked her reputation by making love on the grass? Of course not. She wouldn't make love to anyone unless she was serious about him, and Max Monroe was not going to get serious about her or anyone.

She got up and walked around the house, trying to stay away from the windows that faced his house. She knew she was being silly. Nothing had happened except for a little picnic and a little flirtation. If she were an ordinary woman, accustomed to such things, she'd go back outside, lie in the sun on a chaise lounge in the patio, and give a casual wave to the man across the fence.

Instead she paced around the house like a caged tiger. She needed an excuse to stop working. She was tired of sitting there, staring at the screen, feeling like a different person than the historian who got her biggest kick out of reading, writing and living history.

What had happened to that woman? She'd been replaced by a sex-crazed zombie who wanted a man she couldn't have. Why didn't she lust over one of her colleagues, one who admired her mind? Someone who she could communicate with on an intellectual level.

Why? Because they were dull, dull, dull. Considering all they had in common with her, it was strange that she still had no desire to hang out with them and talk history after work. Talking history with Max was different. Though he claimed to know nothing about the subject, he acted like he was interested in everything she told him.

His interest seemed genuine, and his attention inspired her to make the stories even more interesting. But what if this was all Aunt Mary's doing? What if she'd made sure he knew what would appeal to her? She thought he'd have to be a really good actor to fake the smile on his face, the eager look in his eyes and the questions he asked her.

Still, he didn't have to as far as he had. He didn't have

to give her swimming lessons or kiss her in the park. All he had to do was to be polite. He'd gone way beyond that.

The phone rang and she was grateful for the interruption. She was tired of reading and writing though she'd done precious little of it for the last few days. It seemed the more fun she had, the more fun she wanted to have.

"I just called to see how the presentation went," Trudy said.

Sarah assured her everything had gone well. The kids were well-behaved, they asked good questions and she'd enjoyed it too. "Except for the dress. It was so tight I could hardly breathe."

"Really? I sent it out to be cleaned and it must have shrunk." Her voice trembled.

"Are you all right?" Sarah asked, alarmed. Maybe she was sicker than she'd admitted.

"Actually I…I didn't want to say anything, but…"

"Yes, what is it?" Now Sarah was really worried. Trudy never took any sick leave. She seemed in excellent physical and mental health. She was generous with her time and her praise, but always very professional. Her boss had never discussed anything outside of work with her. But Sarah had seen pictures on her desk of Trudy and her husband and their dog. A perfect family.

Trudy burst into tears on the other end of the phone.

"What's wrong?" Sarah asked, gripping the phone tightly.

"It's Graham. He…he wants a divorce."

"What? But I thought…"

"You thought we had the perfect marriage. So did I. But Graham didn't. He's found someone else—" Trudy broke off and sobbed loudly. When she caught her breath, she continued. "After twenty-seven years. I don't know what to do. What to say. I feel, I've never felt this way before. I'm sorry. I shouldn't be crying on your shoulder, Sarah, after all, it's not your problem."

Sarah was shocked. All this time, all these years she'd worked at the society, Trudy had been the very picture of control, the epitome of calm and serious professionalism. Here she was, calling Sarah and spilling her most private problems. Maybe it was easier to tell someone you worked with rather than a family member or a close friend. Sarah didn't know what to say, except how sorry she was.

She had a million questions to ask. What about money? Do you have a good lawyer? There was a question she could ask, that she *should* ask.

"I haven't talked to a lawyer yet," Trudy said weakly. "It's all been so sudden. I don't want to make things worse by getting a lawyer. Especially not a shark. You know how lawyers are."

Sarah murmured something noncommittal. She only knew one lawyer, and her impression of lawyers was clouded by his personality. He was lively, interesting, interested in her, and very very attractive. He made her feel like a desirable woman. But what was he really like as a lawyer? He was a shark, that much was obvious. He had to be if he was as successful as he seemed.

"The minute you get a lawyer," Trudy continued, "it turns into an adversarial situation. They make demands. And you lose control. The situation gets uncomfortable and maybe even messy. I'm hoping we can work this out. Stay together. If not, I want to be friends, even if the worst happens…even if—" She broke off and Sarah thought she was crying again.

"I understand what you're saying," Sarah said. "But you have to protect yourself. The man next door is a divorce lawyer. He seems very successful. Why don't I ask him…I mean just get his advice. Because if Graham has a lawyer, you don't want to be at a disadvantage." Was that Sarah talking? Sounding like Max himself?

"Don't go out of your way," Trudy mumbled. "I'll be fine. I'm sure I will."

Which just made Sarah more determined to help her boss.

"I'll see what I can find out and I'll call you back," Sarah said.

"Call me on my cell phone. I'm staying at my sister's. I just had to get away. I couldn't stand sleeping in our bed by myself while Graham slept downstairs."

"Of course," Sarah said. Fortunately Trudy had a sister. Then why was she confiding in Sarah? At a time like this, she assumed most people wouldn't be thinking clearly. They needed a friend who wasn't biased. They also needed someone on their side. In other words, they needed a lawyer. Of that Sarah was pretty sure.

But was it self-interest that made her think of offering to ask Max to take Trudy's case? Was she rushing
over to his house because she wanted to see him or was
it really to help Trudy? She didn't bother to mull this
question over. She hung up with a promise to get back
to Trudy right away with something, anything that
might help her.

Then Sarah raced out the back door, into the bright
sunlight, through the gate and up to Max's patio doors
which were wide-open. She stood on the threshold for
a moment, blinking as her eyes got accustomed to the
cool shady interior.

There were voices coming from somewhere inside
the house. In her haste, Sarah had forgotten that Max
had an appointment that afternoon. She stood there,
one hand in the air, ready to knock on the door frame.

"I don't know what to do," a woman said. "I feel
so helpless, so alone. You're the only one I can count
on, Max."

"Now, Arlene, that's not true. You have friends,
family…"

"But I don't have Charlie." Her sobs rang out
through the house.

"I can't bring him back to you."

"I know, I know. What went wrong?"

"I don't know. Do you want me to talk to him?"

"He won't listen. He knows you're on my side. He's
got a lawyer, too. I hate it. I hate it."

"Yes, I know." Max said. "Don't cry, Arlene, I'll do

my best for you." Then there was a long silence. Sarah wondered if Max had put his arms around his client. If he was comforting her. If that was his modus operandi. He was good at hugging and kissing. Sarah knew that much. Did she think she was the only one he hugged? Of course not.

"Thank you, Max. That's all I ask. Because your best is better than anyone else's." The woman's voice was shaky and muffled. Was that because her face was pressed into Max's chest? Was that because he was drying her tears? Or kissing her gently on the lips?

Sarah craned her neck, shamelessly trying to look around to see what was going on. But Max and his client were nowhere to be seen. Probably in the living room. Sarah had no idea what the layout of the house was. He'd never invited her in. Was that deliberate or just that he hadn't had a chance?

She didn't know whether to go or stay. She didn't know how long these conferences lasted. Finally she decided to stay, for Trudy's sake. After all, this was a business call of sorts. Trudy might want to hire Max. If these women were right, and he was the best, she ought to hire him, no matter how much she didn't want to upset the relationship between her and her husband.

Sarah waited until she heard a car pull out of Max's driveway, then she knocked determinedly on the patio door.

"Sarah!" Max, barefoot and in shorts, sounded surprised to see her. As she was equally surprised to see him in such casual clothes. Was this how lawyers met their clients? "Come on in, I just got rid of a client and I'm kind of shaken up. But that's not your problem. I'm glad you're here. I want to talk to you."

"I want to talk to *you*," she said. She remembered the last words he'd said to her. *We have to talk.* Those ominous words that never meant good news. Whatever he had to say, she didn't want to hear it. Not now. "It's business," she added.

"Business?" he asked. "You want to talk about divorce?"

"It's about my boss. Her husband wants a divorce. She doesn't want to get a lawyer. She thinks it will…" She shifted from one foot to the other. "Can we sit down?"

"How about on my patio? Let me get you some iced tea."

Sarah took a seat at his wrought-iron table under the shade of an apple tree. She clasped and unclasped her hands. He wasn't treating this like business, with the casual setting and the glass of tea, but she knew he'd take her request seriously. She knew she could count on him to give good advice. All those women couldn't be wrong.

"Now," he said, setting two glasses on the table. "What's the problem?"

Sarah felt better already, just by looking into his sympathetic, silver-gray eyes. She'd enlist him to help Trudy and Trudy would get the help she needed. "My boss just called to say her husband wants a divorce," she repeated.

"Do you know him?"

"Not really. I've only seen him at meetings. But I can't believe he'd leave her. She's a wonderful boss, a really kind and caring woman, smart, too."

"So she needs a lawyer. Of course I'll take her, Sarah. Any friend of yours…"

"The problem is she doesn't want a lawyer. Not yet anyway. She thinks it will drive a wedge between them, make things uncomfortable, awkward."

"You mean they aren't uncomfortable at this point?"

"I think they must be. She's in shock. Can't believe it's happening to her. They've been married for a long time and she said she wants to stay together. I gather this is all his idea."

"It's not unusual for one person to want to hold on to the marriage," Max said. "One person can be oblivious that anything's wrong."

"You don't know Trudy. She's not oblivious at all. She knows what's going on. She's in charge of our whole department."

"Maybe they'll go into couples' therapy and work things out."

"But you're a divorce lawyer. I assume you make more money if there's a divorce, not a reconciliation."

"You think I'd stand in the way of a couple getting back together?" His mouth tightened. "Just the opposite. Divorces are terrible things, painful things. If you could have heard the woman who was just here…" He paused and took a deep breath. His face was creased with worry lines. "Sometimes a divorce is the lesser of two evils. But not that often. Look, I already have more business than I can handle, Sarah. If she doesn't want a lawyer, and there's hope they'll get back together, she doesn't need me."

"I didn't mean that." Why couldn't she keep her mouth shut? "I'm just afraid he'll take advantage of her. From what I can see, you wouldn't let that happen to any of your clients."

"You're right. I wouldn't. Why don't you sound her out, invite her down here, or I can meet her in town, if she'd prefer. What's her name?"

"Trudy Stewart."

Max frowned. "Her husband's name isn't Graham, is it?"

"Yes, it is. Why? Do you know him?"

"I didn't know him until he called me a few days ago. And I agreed to take his case."

Sarah pushed her chair back from the table and got to her feet. "Oh, no."

"Oh, yes. I'm sorry. If I'd known I would have taken your friend."

"She's not a friend, she's a colleague. But she doesn't deserve to be dumped on. What did he say? Why is he doing this? Is there someone else?"

"I can't tell you. Because of attorney-client privilege."

"Can you tell me if there's a chance of them getting back together?"

"No. Don't ask me, Sarah. There are rules about these things."

"Okay. I'm sorry I asked. I should never have gotten myself involved. Let's pretend I never asked you about it."

"That's exactly right. This is a job for lawyers. Tell your friend to get herself one, too. It's only common sense. You have to make her see that's the only thing she can do."

For once Sarah stifled her impulse to protest, to say something negative about lawyers. She had no business being in the middle of someone else's divorce. She just hated to tell Trudy, "Guess what, your husband has the world's best divorce lawyer. You haven't got a chance."

Forget about getting back together. Forget about getting a decent settlement. Because no matter who your lawyer is, he isn't going to be as good as Max Monroe. I can tell.

Then Trudy would just give up and accept the inevitable and hire someone else, someone who'd try to get what she deserved for her, but it would be a losing battle.

"I'm sorry," Sarah said, trying to keep a stiff upper lip.

"I'm sorry, too. Just so you know, I have no personal interest in this case the way you do. But I've taken this man's case. You may think I have no scruples, but believe me I do. He's my client and I represent him."

Sarah's face flushed, she was so angry. She turned and stomped all the way to her aunt's house. She felt like a fool, first offering Max to her boss, then finding out he'd already been hired by her husband. Well, Sarah was going to make sure Trudy got what she deserved. Max might be good, but was he really the best? In any case, he wasn't the only good divorce lawyer in town. Sarah was going to find one for Trudy who'd fight for her and win. Scruples? She'd show Max Monroe who had scruples!

Chapter Eleven

"Aunt Mary! What are you doing here?"

She wasn't supposed to be back until the end of the week, but there she was, standing in the middle of her living room, surrounded by her luggage, looking tanned and fit.

"There was an outbreak of one of those viruses on board," the petite, silver-haired woman said, hugging her niece. "Don't worry, I didn't get it."

"Why didn't you call? I would have picked you up. How did you get here from the airport?"

"Oh, I took the shuttle. I called but you didn't answer so I assumed you were out, and I didn't want to bother you. It all happened so suddenly. When people started getting sick, they canceled the cruise, and flew

us home from Puerto Rico. Silly me, I don't have one
of those cell phones and I never had a moment to get
to a pay phone. I hope you're not disappointed. Don't
think you have to rush off. You planned to be here all
week. I hope you'll stick around. We need to have some
time together."

Disappointed? No, Sarah was relieved. Now her aunt
could use her own opera tickets. Sarah would have the
perfect excuse for not going with Max. It was time to
make a break from him. Right now. Every time she saw
him she got more and more involved. She had no right
to disapprove of his profession. Or how he chose his clients. She had no right to ask favors of him. She had no
business kissing him or letting him kiss her. She was not
the type for a summer romance. Before she met him she
was happy and content. Well, perhaps a little restless,
but still, her life was complete. And now? All she
needed to do was to get back to the city and everything
else would fall into place. This summer would fade like
a dream.

Stick around? No way. Her aunt couldn't have come
back at a better time. It was time to leave before she got
any more involved than she was, because she was head-
ing for a broken heart.

"How is everything here?" her aunt asked anxiously,
when Sarah didn't respond. She put her hands on her
hips and surveyed her niece. "You look like you got a
little sunshine."

Sarah shook herself from her reverie. In her mind she

was already packed and on her way back to her real life. "Oh, yes. The weather's been great."

"Well, good. All the more reason to enjoy the house and summer out of the city. You must stay the week as planned."

"I really should get back," Sarah murmured. "My boss has been sick." Now Sarah realized Trudy hadn't been sick at all, merely sick at heart over the breakdown of her marriage. Who wouldn't feel sick under those circumstances?

"But you deserve a vacation. I'm sure they can manage a few more days without you. Besides, I was hoping you could help me buy a computer, like the little portable one you have. I realized on my trip that I need to update myself. Just because I'm old doesn't mean I have to act old. I want a computer and I want a cell phone. I played bridge with a man on board who's miles ahead of me in the world of technology. Of course that's not saying much since I'm at ground zero. Not a bad dancer, either. Then there are the opera tickets."

"Now that you're back, you can go," Sarah said hopefully.

"Oh, no, I've got jet lag. I'd never make it through three acts. You go. You take a friend and go."

Sarah opened her mouth to protest, but it was no use when her aunt was determined, and she most definitely was.

"Well, it sounds like you had a great time," Sarah said, dropping the opera question for the moment.

"Yes, too bad it had to end so soon. I thought we might…never mind. I had lots of fun. More fun than anyone my age has a right to. But back to my lack of digital equipment. If I had a computer I could e-mail my new friend, I mean friends." If Sarah didn't know better, she might have thought her aunt was blushing. "I thought we'd go shopping. If you have time, that is."

"Shopping? Aren't you tired? You just flew in from Puerto Rico. I thought you had jet lag."

"I don't mean now. You're right, I am tired. What time is it?" She looked at her watch. "I'm so confused. We'll go tomorrow, if you don't mind, that is." She started up the stairs, then paused. "Did you have a chance to meet my neighbor, Max?"

Sarah stiffened. Here it came. The sixty-four-thousand-dollar question. "Yes, I did."

"And?"

"And he was very nice. I don't think he ever intended to cut down your tree, if that's what you were worried about."

"That and other things," her aunt said softly.

"What about dinner? Would you like me to fix you something?" Sarah asked.

"Oh, no, I had something on the plane." She smiled and yawned. "I'm exhausted. I'll take a little nap and we'll talk later. About the opera…"

"Yes?"

"If you haven't asked anyone yet, we could ask Max to go with you."

"Right," Sarah said weakly. What else could she say? He was planning on going with her, her aunt didn't know that, so she could hardly back out now. And after the opera, after she'd left, what would Max tell her aunt about her? What would she tell her aunt about Max? Nothing, that's what. She'd just said it all. Restlessly she paced around the house, not wanting to go outside for fear of seeing him, not wanting to go upstairs to the guest room for fear of disturbing her aunt and knowing she wouldn't be able to sleep. Not now. She'd only toss and turn.

Sarah could not walk out of the house and return to the city now, as much as she wanted to. Aunt Mary was such a trooper, so determined not to grow old before her time that Sarah had to encourage her by taking her shopping for a computer and a cell phone tomorrow.

As she was fixing herself a cup of tea, the phone rang and a man asked for Mary. Sarah said she'd gone to bed. The man laughed and said he thought she needed some sleep after that cruise. Sarah took his name and number and after she hung up she had a good idea that it might be the man Aunt Mary had danced and played Bridge with. The same man who'd inspired her to go high tech. Sarah smiled to herself. He must be quite a man!

That evening Max walked around his garden, inhaling the fresh air, admiring his sparkling pool and casting curious glances at the house next door. He'd heard

voices, but had no idea who was talking to Sarah. He
wished she'd come out of the house. He didn't want to
go over there and knock on the door yet again. Though
maybe it was his turn to take the initiative. He wanted
Sarah to like him. Why? What did it matter? She'd be
gone out of his neighborhood and out of his life in a few
days.

He didn't know why it mattered so much, they had
absolutely no future together, but it did matter. He kept
visualizing those big blue eyes of hers gazing at him as
she told him stories. He remembered how she felt in his
arms in the pool, so warm, so innocent, so trusting that
he wouldn't let her go.

Now what? They'd go to the opera and then she'd
go back to her real life and he'd stay right where he was
and where he wanted to be. He hoped Sarah understood
why he did what he did and that he never intended to
gouge anyone. All he ever wanted was for his clients to
get what was coming to them. A fair and equal settlement. What was wrong with that?

What was wrong was that someone always got hurt.
Sometimes both parties got hurt. He saw it happen. He
saw it happen today. The tears, the sense of betrayal,
the loss. Sometimes it took his clients years to get over
it, despite how spunky and upbeat they acted. Under-
neath they were hurting. He knew that. But what was
the answer? His parents certainly didn't have the answer.

He strolled around the garden, restless, his mind going around in circles, trying to think of a way out. He walked back to the fragrant eucalyptus trees where he'd first seen Sarah that night, only a few nights ago, but it seemed like a long time. He wished she'd reappear in her nightgown and he could take her in his arms and tell her...tell her what?

Tell her he didn't want her to leave. He liked having her around. He wanted her to stay, not go back to the city. They'd only begun to get to know each other. He sensed there might be more there than just a casual flirtation or friendship. Not that he'd ever want anything permanent, of course. It would take more than a few kisses to convince him to ever get married.

Married? Where did that come from? He had to make it clear to her that the good times they were having were just that. It's what he would have said before he let her out of the car after their picnic. He didn't want her to get the wrong idea. She was vulnerable and had had little practice on the dating scene. That much he knew.

He picked up a few eucalyptus nuts from the ground and rolled them around in his palm. The faintly medicinal smell reminded him of her. He remembered how she looked in her bed that first night. Her pale face framed with her dark hair against the pillow. It was a sight he'd never forget.

He wandered around the place some more, thinking of all the clients he'd had, the rich and not-so-rich, the betrayed and the betrayers, the hopeful and the hopeless and he wondered what the answer was. The answer? He didn't even know what the question was.

He wandered until it was dark, and later in the evening he saw the lights go off all over the house next door. He waited for a few more hours, thinking maybe this was the night she'd sleepwalk again, but nothing happened. He was not disappointed. Of course not. He just wanted to be there in case she did walk and needed help getting back home again.

The next morning he hurried outside again. He wanted to talk to Sarah, to explain once again how the legal system worked and why he did what he did, before he forgot all the reasons he'd come up with. But he didn't want to go up and knock on the door again. That was getting old. But the woman outside in the garden next door was Mary, not Sarah.

"Aren't you back early?" he asked, coming to the fence. What did it mean? Would Sarah leave now? He had a sinking feeling in the pit of his stomach that she'd already left. Without so much as a goodbye. That hurt.

"Yes, I got back yesterday. It was that nasty virus that swept through the ship." She held up her hand. "I didn't get it, thank heavens, but enough of the other passengers did that they canceled the cruise. I got a free ticket to another one and a free ride home, so no harm done," she said cheerfully. "I understand you and Sarah have met."

What had she said about him? "Yes, she's an interesting girl," he said carefully.

Mary beamed. "Isn't she? Of all my nieces and nephews she's my favorite. She's done remarkably well considering the way she was raised which I don't mind telling you I did not approve of. In any case, she's turned out well, smart and kind and just lovely. All she needs is…well, nothing. Did I tell you she's taking me shopping today? One thing I learned on my cruise is that I'm not keeping up with the times. I don't have a computer or a cell phone. Today I'm buying one of each."

"Then Sarah's not leaving right away," he said, his heart ratcheting against his ribs while he tried to sound casual. He was relieved. Maybe there was still a chance to redeem himself, to talk to her, to say something, although he didn't know what or how.

"Oh, no, she wouldn't do that," Mary said. "For one thing, she's going to use my opera tickets Friday night."

"I know. She offered me the other one."

Mary's eyes widened. "Really? Well that's a wonderful idea. I think I'd better get back to the house and make sure she has the appropriate outfit. Some of her clothes are on the casual side, I've noticed."

Max hid a smile. "Yes, I've noticed, too."

There, that ought to do it, Max thought. No way was Sarah going to get out of going to the opera with him on Friday. Not with her aunt's seal of approval on the event.

He didn't see her again until then. He was busy seeing clients, calling other lawyers, trying to get them to take over some of his cases. He didn't know if he could really unload his whole list, he just knew the divorce business, as he currently practiced it, left him feeling empty and dissatisfied. Whose fault was that? Was it Lila? Her husband? Or was it the accumulation of all the Lilas in the past and all their husbands?

He didn't know. How long had it been coming on? He couldn't say. The only thing he knew for sure was that any time he'd had a bad feeling about his job in the past, he reminded himself how it felt to be poor. He was stuck between a rock and a hard place. He didn't want to handle any more greedy clients and he didn't want to have to sell his house, either, or live from hand-to-mouth. There had to be another way to make a living. Employment law? Property law? He'd have to start at the bottom of a big firm.

He traveled up to the city, then down to the courthouse. He pushed and he pulled to get what he thought his clients deserved. He tried persuasion and he tried bullying. Somehow he hammered out agreements faster and more thoroughly than ever before. Not everyone was happy with his or her settlement. But that was the name of the game. He did his best. He tried to do what was fair.

He felt motivated as he never was before. He had been nudged out of his routine by his meeting Sarah and seeing the contrast between her and the people at his party. She was happy in her own skin, they were not. She was not looking for someone to make her life complete, they were.

He didn't know where this change was leading, but something would happen. He signed up for some psychology classes, maybe the answer would be there.

On Friday he left a message on Mary's phone that he'd be by at five to pick up Sarah for dinner and the opera. He was glad she didn't answer the phone because he could just hear her now.

Dinner? I thought it was just the opera. Opera? I forgot all about it. I can't go. I have nothing to wear. But when he went to Mary's front door Sarah answered the door. Nothing to wear? She'd found something to wear all right.

She was wearing a black dress that hugged her slender figure and showed off her long legs and smooth skin. He stood and stared for a long moment until she finally asked if something was wrong.

"Wrong?" Something was very right. "You look different. Great, I mean. I've never seen you in a dress before, that is a modern-day dress."

"It's new," Sarah said, feeling her cheeks flush. She didn't look like herself and she didn't feel like herself. But the look in Max's eyes told her she'd done something right. Aunt Mary told her, too. "Aunt Mary bought it for me. The shoes, too." She stepped back into the room and Max walked in.

"You look different, too," she said. Different? He looked sensational, the white shirt and dark tie made him look drop-dead gorgeous. "I...I've never seen you in a suit."

"I do wear one occasionally."

Sarah took her coat from the closet. She felt strange and it wasn't just the dress or his suit. It was something in the air. A change in their relationship. It was like a date, but it wasn't. Not at all. They were almost out the door when her aunt came down the stairs.

"Have a wonderful time, you two," she said, her eyes twinkling. If only Aunt Mary didn't expect so much of her. She wanted something to work out between her and her neighbor. Sarah knew this from various remarks Aunt Mary had made this week. Sarah had done her best to head her off. But Aunt Mary was a very determined woman. Oh, well, soon Sarah would be gone and Aunt Mary would have to deal with her failure as a matchmaker.

Sarah didn't think she'd have anything to say on the way to the city. But Max had questions about the history of San Francisco itself and of course Sarah had answers. Max chuckled at her descriptions of the colorful characters, some famous like Mark Twain, some not as famous like Emperor Norton. As before, he made her feel witty and charming. He also made her feel beautiful by the look in his eyes.

They had dinner at a small French bistro on Geary Street that Max knew about. It was the kind of place Sarah had never been to, with white tablecloths and candles. The kind of place that said romance in a very subtle way.

Over Coquilles St. Jacques and baby French green

beans, Sarah turned the tables on Max and asked questions about his work. This time he told stories about his clients, withholding all names of course, that gave her an insight into human nature she'd never had before. She also had an insight into Max's talent at reconciliation.

"I don't know how you do it," she said, sipping her sparkling white wine appreciatively. "Keeping everyone happy."

"I don't," he said soberly. "I can't do it anymore."

"What?" she asked. "You're not going to quit, are you?"

"I can't quit, but…"

Just then the waiter came with their dessert, tiny profiteroles covered with chocolate sauce.

"You were saying," Sarah reminded him when the waiter had left.

"Nothing. I have no answers. I just have a dilemma." Then he changed the subject without saying exactly what the dilemma was.

By the time they got to the opera, and climbed the steps to the massive open doors, with Max's hand on her arm, she was feeling like she'd ascended into a rarified world along with the other patrons.

As they stood in line to get in, they couldn't help overhearing a young couple at the ticket window asking for five-dollar standing room tickets. When they were told they had no more, the girl turned and they saw tears of disappointment in her eyes. Her boyfriend put one arm around her shoulders to comfort her. Max looked at Sarah and she looked at him. He lifted one eyebrow. She nodded.

Sarah walked over to the couple and held out her tickets. "Would you like these?" she asked.

The girl stared at her as if she had told her she'd won the lottery. "I...we can't afford them," she said, blinking rapidly.

"They're a gift. From my aunt Mary. She'd want you to have them."

The young man broke into a huge smile. "Are you sure you don't want them?" he asked Max.

"Sure. We can go another time. And besides, we have a lot to talk about. It's hard to talk during an opera."

Max took Sarah's hand and left the couple looking dazed and delighted.

"I'll never forget the looks on their faces," Sarah said. "I wish Aunt Mary could have seen them."

"We'll tell her about it," he said. "Now, what shall we do?"

"I've never been to Pier 39."

"I've never ridden a cable car," Max said.

"I feel like I've been given the night off," Sarah said. She felt giddy and silly. It must be the wine, she told herself. But of course it was Max. It was the night. And it was the city.

They rode the cable car, standing on the outside and hanging on to the railing, they laughed, they talked, they held hands and walked from one end of Fisherman's Wharf to the other, mingling with tourists and locals alike.

By the time they stopped for Irish coffee, got back in their car and headed home to the suburbs it was midnight.

"It's a good thing I'm going back to work soon or I could become completely spoiled," she said, settling back into the leather seat of Max's sports car. She wouldn't let herself think about ending these good times. But they would end, and end very soon.

"When will that be?" he asked.

"Just a few more days," she said, and quite suddenly was overcome with a feeling of sadness. It was over. Really over. Just in time. Before she fell in love with a man she couldn't have.

After talking nonstop for hours it seemed, Sarah didn't know what to say on the way home. She had to prepare herself for real life. As for Max, he was uncharacteristically quiet, too. He seemed to have run out of questions to ask her or stories to tell about outrageous clients.

He parked in his driveway and walked her to her aunt's front door. There he kissed her lightly on the mouth under the porch light.

"I hope you're not sorry we missed the opera," he said, brushing his thumb over her cheek.

She felt chills all over her arms and it had nothing to do with the cool evening air.

"Not at all. I had a good time. A really good time."

"So did I. Just because you're going back to work, there's no reason why we can't continue to see each other. I'd like to get to know you better, Sarah."

"It's been fun," she said. She knew that wasn't what he wanted to hear, but what could she say? I'm afraid to get to know you any better? Being with you makes me want more than I can have. I know who you are and you know who I am and you know we have no future together. You're gun-shy. You've got a suit of protective armor and you never get serious about anyone. I can't deal with that. I'm a serious person. After a night like tonight she wanted to tell him it had been fantastic, that she wanted more of the same, just as he did, maybe even more than he did, but what was the point?

"Fun?" he said. "Is that all you can say?"

"Max, let's be realistic. We live in two different worlds. Not just geographically. But we want different things from life. You're a lawyer, a confirmed bachelor with a completely different lifestyle."

"And you're a confirmed scholar. Why can't our two worlds overlap?" he asked, tucking a strand of hair behind her ears. "Why can't we continue as we're doing? Nights on the town? Overnights on the town?" he asked with a suggestive glint in his eyes.

His touch was unbearably sweet. But his words made her feel cold all over. He wanted to have an affair with her. She wanted more. He made her want more than just the life of a scholar. But less than a fling. It made her want love and marriage. Whoa. She was getting way ahead of herself. He'd told her plainly he didn't want to get married.

"You don't know me, not really," she said.

"I think I do. I think I know you pretty well. I want to get to know you better," he said. "What's wrong with that?"

"It won't lead anywhere," she said.

"How do you know unless we try?"

"I just know. You've made it clear how you feel about love and marriage." There she said it. Not only had he made it clear, she'd heard it from others. If he had any sense he'd know she was not the type for an affair. She'd had no experience with men. He was the first man she'd ever fallen for. It had taken years for her to let down her guard. When this didn't work out, how long would it take for her to put her guard back up? A lifetime? No, it wasn't worth it. She had to end it now while she still had her wits about her and her life ahead of her. The life of a scholar.

"Are you saying that's what you want? Promises? Forever after?"

She felt her face turning red, fortunately he wouldn't notice in the dim porch light. "I…I'm not sure. Please don't misunderstand. All I'm saying is that we've had a good time, but it wasn't meant to last. I have a life, so do you. Let's agree to go back to where we came from."

"Just like that?" he asked, his mouth twisted in a frown.

"Yes, just like that." She was proud of how light-hearted she sounded when inside she felt like she swallowed a cube of ice.

"I'm sorry you feel that way," he said. "But I'm not taking no for an answer." Then he turned and left.

Sarah went in the house and collapsed on the sofa. Fortunately her aunt had gone to bed and couldn't see the tears that shook her. She buried her face in a throw pillow and sobbed. When she finally stopped, she told herself that even though Max was used to getting what he wanted, this time she'd stand firm. She had her own happiness, her peace of mind to preserve. If only she were a different woman and he was a different man then maybe she'd agree. Let's date, let's have an affair, she'd say. But she wasn't and she couldn't say that.

How could two people be more different than they were? It was time to end this relationship, if you could call it that, and get back to real life. It was time to stop dreaming. Sarah blew her nose, took off the black dress and went to bed. But not to sleep. Not to sleepwalk, either. She lay there wide-awake, plotting her return to the city.

The next day Sarah and her aunt were on their way out of the computer store with a top-of-the-line laptop computer with all the bells and whistles and a brand-new cell phone. That was when she got up enough nerve to tell her aunt she had to go home to the city. Then and now.

Mary looked puzzled and disappointed. "Is it something I've done?" she asked.

Sarah managed a smile. "Of course not. I love being here with you, it's just…"

"Does this have something to do with Max?"

Sarah felt the heat rise to her face. "I like him a lot, Aunt Mary," she said, tired of keeping it to herself. "I'm afraid I like him too much."

"Nonsense. How can that be?"

"I'm not the type for a casual flirtation."

"Of course not," her aunt said, standing in the middle of the parking lot with the computer in a cart in front of her. "Is he?"

Sarah nodded. "I'm afraid so. He's made it quite clear he's not cut out for marriage. I don't blame him, not after what he's seen as a divorce attorney. And not that he'd want to marry me even if he was interested in marriage. I barely know him. I went to his party, I had dinner with him one night, and a picnic another time, he came to my presentation, then he gave me a few swimming lessons and then the opera which we didn't see."

"Hmm," her aunt said. "I had no idea you'd spent so much time together."

"We didn't. I mean, it seems like more than it was. What I learned about him is that his job has contributed to his outlook on life. As my job has to mine. I can't change that."

"So you're determined to leave and not see him

again, ever?" her aunt asked, her forehead creased, her mouth turned down at the corners.

"Don't say it like that, Aunt Mary. I'm determined to do what's best for me and for him. Is that so wrong?"

Once they unloaded the new equipment into her car, her aunt gave her a hug and answered her question.

"Of course it's not wrong, dear. You do what you have to do. Before you get your heart broken," her aunt said. "I understand completely. And I feel somewhat responsible."

"Not at all. You mustn't blame yourself."

"But I thought, I even hoped…"

"I know. Now let's pretend I never mentioned it. And I hope you'll explain to Max that I left because of my work and not because of him."

Her aunt nodded soberly and was quiet during the ride back to her house. After they spent the afternoon setting up Aunt Mary's computer and programming her cell phone, Sarah packed her bags and left early the next morning. She deliberately avoided glancing at the house next door, not even a peek in the rearview mirror as she drove down the street. But she couldn't help the tears that streamed down her face as she drove away.

She told herself she was crying because a brief interlude in her life was over. Not because she'd fallen in love with a man she couldn't have. This wasn't love. It couldn't be. You couldn't love someone you scarcely knew.

She was on her way home, back where she belonged, where there would be nothing to remind her of Max.

* * *

Max heard her car start that morning and watched her leave from the window upstairs. So she was gone out of his life. Before he'd had a chance to tell her how special she was, how different from any other woman he'd ever known. He wondered if he'd ever get tired of hearing her stories, if he'd ever get tired of watching the color rise in her cheeks when she got excited or embarrassed. Would he ever get tired of looking at her, whether in a swimsuit, nightgown or long historical dress?

The idea of never seeing her again made him feel empty inside. Why? He'd been happy before she came, he'd be happy now that she was gone, wouldn't he? Just as soon as he got used to the idea. He didn't know what was wrong with him. He'd never felt this way before, as if he was losing something precious.

For the rest of the summer she wouldn't be hanging around the patio in her swimsuit, she wouldn't be next door working on her computer, her attention focused on her work.

He wouldn't see her face light up as she described the characters out of the past. He wouldn't hear the enthusiasm in her voice as she painted word pictures of life in California as it once was. He wouldn't be able to just knock on her door when he felt like it.

What was so wrong with seeing her in the city? She'd sure put the kibosh on that idea. He'd pictured himself going to the Mission Dolores and having her explain it to him, or visiting one of the old schooners anchored in the Bay with her leading the way down the narrow steps to the galley. The city was full of historical sites that he had an unquenchable desire to see and hear more about.

There were picnic spots, too, Golden Gate Park, for example, or Ocean Beach or the Marina Green. All of which he'd seen, but not with Sarah. Where they could lie on the grass or the sand and munch on bread and cheese and fresh fruit. There was a whole world out there he wanted to explore with her. But she said it was over. She wouldn't see him. She'd made that clear. Only he didn't accept it. He'd told her he wouldn't take no for an answer and he meant it. He didn't get where he was by giving in too soon.

Chapter Twelve

Sarah was working hard on her speech for the historical society. If she thought it would be easy to concentrate once she got back to the city, she was wrong. Two weeks had gone by and still her mind constantly wandered back to the house next door to Max's. She was glad to have a lot of work to do. It kept her mind off the events of those few days she'd spent with Max. She hadn't heard from him. She didn't expect to. She'd spoken to her aunt a few times but neither one had mentioned her handsome neighbor. What was there to say, after all? She didn't want her aunt to think she'd fallen in love with a man who was so wrong for her.

Aunt Mary would feel bad, maybe even guilty for asking her to house-sit and for asking him to look out for her. Besides, what made her think she'd fallen in love? How did she know what falling in love felt like? How did she know what it was that made her mood swings so violent, sometimes giddy with the memories of Max and the good times, other times plunged into despair at the realization that those good times were gone forever and that it had been her decision to end it so abruptly.

By the next week she was as prepared as she could possibly be with a speech on the Gold Rush. It was a subject she knew quite well and enjoyed talking about. It was also popular with the general public, more popular than say, talking about the missionary period. The lecture had been advertised in the local papers and the hall at the society was full that Saturday morning.

Sarah spread her notes in front of her and checked with the man who would project the photographs onto the screen from his computer in the back of the room. Her boss Trudy met her in the hall before introducing her.

"Sarah, we have to talk," she said, taking Sarah's arm and clutching it tightly.

"Is it…how is everything going?" Sarah asked, searching the older woman's face for tearstains or dark circles under her eyes. She hadn't seen her for weeks. Trudy had called in to say she was taking some time off and would Sarah be able to handle some of the administrative work while she was out.

Sarah assured her it was no problem and then reluctantly told her the bad news that Max wouldn't be able to take her case. When she offered to find her another hotshot lawyer, Trudy turned her down flat. Sarah was relieved to see that today Trudy looked as if she was back to normal. She wore a smart black pantsuit and a silk blouse. Sarah concluded she must have found herself a lawyer without Sarah's help.

"I'll explain later," Trudy said in a low voice.

Sarah had a moment to look around the room and smile at the familiar faces in the audience. One was her aunt who was in the third row, beaming proudly at her, others were colleagues or friends. Her parents were in the last row. She'd only spoken briefly to them since she'd been back. When they called she begged off, saying she was too busy to talk. She was afraid they'd get onto the subject of her swimming lessons or some other worry over her health, and she no longer had the time nor inclination to argue with anyone, especially them.

She gave her introduction, beginning with the discovery of gold at Sutter's Mill when she looked up and saw Max standing in the back of the room. Her heart caught in her throat. She stumbled over a word or two then caught herself. What was he doing there? Had her aunt told him about it?

She forced herself to look away. She looked at anyone and everyone else and made herself concentrate on her subject. It wasn't easy but she did it and after the talk, the applause was loud and long. She breathed a huge sigh of relief and answered questions from the floor. She tried not to seek out Max at the back of the room, but she couldn't help catching his gaze. Just once and then she looked away. She wanted to see him, talk to him, and just hear his voice again, but she would never approach him. She didn't know what she'd say. She was afraid she'd break down and fall apart, just when she'd spent a month getting over him. She tried to remember why it was she had to break things off. Oh, yes, it was…no future. Too different. Her health problems. His job. His attitude toward love and marriage. He'd said he wouldn't take no for an answer, but obviously he had.

After the talk and the questions she was immediately surrounded by friends and colleagues who all said nice things about her speech. The next time she looked around, she didn't see Max at all. Her heart sank. He was gone. She'd never see him again. Then why had he come, if he didn't want to talk to her?

"Aunt Mary, how good of you to come," she said after her aunt, looking lovely in a beige wool Chanel suit, hugged her.

"I wouldn't miss it. You were wonderful."

"I thought I saw Max at the back of the room."

Mary turned around. "I wouldn't be surprised. I told him about the talk."

But where is he now? Why didn't he stay? If he didn't want to talk to me, why did he come?

After most of the audience had left, and Max had

never reappeared, she greeted her parents who were waiting for a chance to talk to her.

"How are you, dear?" her mother asked anxiously. "We've been worried about you. You aren't doing anything dangerous, are you?"

"Nothing dangerous at all," Sarah said firmly. "I'm making good progress swimming."

"But I thought…" her mother began, chewing on her lip and frowning at Sarah.

"You thought I couldn't do it, but I can. I've been taking lessons at the Y here in the city, and you'd be amazed at my progress. Oh, my backstroke is still weak and my freestyle…you wouldn't want to see that. But my teacher says I'm ready to go off the high diving board. Then one day I might even join the polar bear club, get a wet suit and swim in the Bay."

Her mother gasped. Her father opened his mouth to protest, but she didn't let him. She kept talking about her plans until they gave up and said goodbye. A goodbye to the old Sarah, one who never took chances, one who was afraid to fall in the water and especially afraid to fall in love.

No more. Buoyed by the enthusiastic reception of her speech, encouraged that Max had come to hear it, even though he'd disappeared as fast as he'd appeared, she was going to take matters into her own hands. Maybe she wasn't the type for an affair, but she knew now she loved him. It was up to her to do something about it. But what?

Gathering her notes and stuffing them into her briefcase, she looked around to see Trudy waiting for her at the door to the hall.

"Sarah, I'm sorry I've been out so much. You've had to do all my work and yours, too."

"It was no problem," Sarah assured her. "Maybe I shouldn't ask, but how are things with you and Graham?"

"Much better. Not that we're getting back together. After I left the house and pulled myself together, I realized that things hadn't been good for a long time. It was almost a relief to have him out of my life. He's a very judgmental person and perhaps I was tired of being judged. Now I do whatever I want, when I want to do it. I know I must have sounded like a basket case when I called you, but I was in shock. When the shock wore off, I decided that life could still go on. What I want to say is that Graham fired his lawyer and we're dealing with a mediator."

Sarah set her briefcase down on a chair. "What? How does that work?"

"It saves us a lot of money for one thing. And for another, there's no bitterness, no recriminations and it's fair. Because the mediator doesn't take sides."

"He must be a saint," Sarah muttered.

"No, he isn't. He's a very attractive man. You'll have to meet him. Or are you seeing someone?"

"No, not really. Not now."

Sarah's knees suddenly buckled and she sat down on a folding chair. What had happened? Did Max blame her for his getting fired as Graham's lawyer? Was that why he didn't stick around after the talk? Was that why he'd never called her?

"Are you okay, Sarah?"

"I'm fine. It's just a little letdown. I got keyed up over my talk and now it's over. Time to get back to work."

"Don't work too hard, Sarah. That's what I learned during my hiatus. I'll be back on Monday and you can take some time off."

"Hmm. Yes, maybe I will. There is something I have to do. Some loose ends to tie up."

Sarah turned to leave, feeling relieved about Trudy, but disappointed about Max, when he suddenly appeared at her side.

"You gave a great talk, no big surprise there," he said soberly.

She smiled. "I'm so glad you stayed. I thought...I thought you'd left."

"I had to congratulate you."

"I want to tell you something. Do you have a minute?"

He nodded. "I've got something to tell you, too."

"I changed my mind." So what if he wasn't looking for love and marriage. She'd take what she could get, because whatever it was, it was better than nothing.

"What?"

"Yes, I want to get to know you. I want to see if..."

"If there's something there between us. There is, Sarah, I know it. I've missed you so much." He hugged her so tightly, she dropped her notes and her briefcase. Neither one noticed. "When should we start getting to know each other? Because I haven't got much time. I'm thirty-five years old and I want a future with you."

"What?" Her knees were so weak she sank into one of the folding chairs.

"I won't press you for an answer now, but I just want to warn you, I'm serious."

"What happened?" she asked. "What happened to your suit of armor, your determination to avoid any entanglements."

"You happened," he said simply.

"Then how about getting started now?" she asked, feeling like laughing and crying at the same time.

He grinned at her, then bent down to kiss her. A kiss that said it all. I want you. I love you. Then he picked up her notes and her briefcase and carried them out for her.

Over coffee she said Trudy told her that Graham had fired his lawyer. "That's you, right?"

"That *was* me. But this week I've been in the city taking classes in mediation and I'm going to hang up a new shingle—Max Monroe, Mediator."

Sarah set her cup down with a bang. "I don't believe it. You're a mediator?"

"It's so much less stress," he said. "I feel like I'm helping both parties, instead of taking sides."

"But what about the money?"

"I'll do fine," he said. "It seems mediators are in big demand. It makes sense. I'm not licensed yet. I have two weeks left to go. While I'm here I want to see you every night and every day. How does that work for you?"

"Let's see, I work during the day and my swimming lessons are at noon, but I'm free in the evenings."

"Swimming lessons? Someone else is teaching you to swim?"

"Just perfecting my stroke, so I can show off."

"I look forward to that," he said, with a huge smile on his face.

Three weeks later

Once again there was a light breeze and a full moon over Max Monroe's house in the quiet suburb of Vista Valley, California. Once again Max stood on his patio smoking a cigar and pondering the past and the future. A future, he had to admit that worried him right now.

He'd made major changes in his life over the past month, but still there was a gaping hole in the middle of it. After two weeks in the city seeing Sarah every evening, he'd felt more and more sure with every day that he was on the right track at last, both personally and professionally.

His classes went well, and more important he and Sarah grew closer. Every evening he'd picked her up from work at the historical society and they'd go somewhere different, take a walk around Chinatown and eat a bowl of noodles at a tiny hole-in-the-wall restaurant or climb the Filbert Steps to the top of Coit Tower, then get takeout and eat at her place.

They laughed and talked and grew so close, Max felt

confident enough to buy a ring and had it in his pocket on his last night in San Francisco. He took her to dinner at a little Italian restaurant in North Beach where he ordered champagne.

"Champagne?" she said, her eyes bright and her cheeks flushed. "Oh, I know, we're celebrating your new career." She held her glass up and tapped it with his.

"That's not all. There's something else I want to celebrate. I love you, Sarah, I want to marry you."

Her eyes widened. "But, Max…"

"I know, I know." He reached for her hand across the table, and held it tightly as if he was afraid she might get away. "All that talk about avoiding marriage so I could avoid divorce. But that was the old Max talking. The new Max is a believer. A believer in love and marriage…with you. If I hadn't met you, I might still be battling lawyers and ex-wives and husbands in court."

"Max, I…I don't know what to say."

"Say yes. Say you love me too. Say you want to spend the rest of your life with me. Say you want to have children with me. You'll teach them about history and I'll teach them to swim and…"

"Wait, wait," Sarah said, her lower lip quivering. "I thought I'd told you. I don't know if I can have children. Because of my asthma."

"But you're fine. You haven't had an attack in how long?"

"A few years. I know. But that's because I've been careful."

"Careful? You've almost drowned, you work hard and you're taking swimming lessons and still you haven't had an attack."

"That's right, but pregnancy is different. There are hormonal changes that happen during pregnancy that can effect the nose, sinuses and lungs. I've read a lot about asthma and I know what I can do and what I can't. That's why I don't know if I'd want to chance getting pregnant. Asthma can cause serious complications like high blood pressure, toxemia and premature delivery."

"Then we'll adopt. I don't care. I want you, Sarah. If you don't feel the same, if you don't love me, tell me now and I'll drop it."

He stared at her, his heart sinking. Could he really be the only one here who'd fallen in love? Could he have mistaken her interest in him for something else? Just interest, that's all?

Her eyes filled with tears. "I do love you, Max. I can't deny it. I've never felt this way before. You've changed the way I feel about life and about myself. I want to marry you and spend the rest of my life with you, but it wouldn't be fair to you. You should have kids, your own kids, kids who will look like you and…"

"Stop. I don't care about that."

"Maybe not now. But you will some day. Please don't make this any harder than it is."

He pressed his lips together to keep from blurting out something he'd regret. "Okay," he said. "You know how I feel. If you change your mind, you know where to find me."

She nodded and wiped a tear from her cheek. He took her home. Neither one of them said very much. He kissed her goodbye, and left the city to go home to his Portola Valley house. And that evening was the last time he'd seen her or heard from her.

So he was waiting. Waiting for what? For her to make up her mind. For her to realize how much he wanted her. How much he loved her. How much he needed her. He was prepared to wait a long time. But not forever.

He hadn't been sleeping well lately. Maybe that's what caused him to see the mysterious figure at the back of his garden under the trees. Afraid to believe what he'd seen, he closed his eyes and hit the side of his head with his palm. When he opened his eyes, the creature was still there, her gown billowing in the breeze.

It couldn't be. It couldn't be her. She was far away in the city. Unless she'd sleepwalked all the way here. No, it must be his imagination. He stubbed out his cigar and walked slowly and quietly toward the vision. When he got up close his heart stopped beating for a long, long moment. It was Sarah, looking so unbelievably beautiful he thought he must be dreaming. Her hair was dark and soft, her skin was pale as alabaster in the moonlight. Her gown was so sheer he could see her creamy breasts and beautiful body as if she was wearing nothing. It was a dream come true.

He was afraid to speak. Afraid to break the spell she was under. More afraid to break the spell *he* was under. Instead he put his hands on her shoulders and bent forward to kiss her.

At the first touch of his lips, Sarah drew in a short breath of surprise. He nibbled at her lips, so gently, so softly, she thought she might die of happiness right there on the spot. Even before she'd said what she'd come to say.

Then he deepened the kiss and she threw her arms around him to answer with kisses of her own.

"Sarah, Sarah," he murmured, his lips against her cheek. "You're not asleep. You came back." He pulled her close and she clung to him as if she'd never let him go. He felt so warm, so solid, so real. He pulled back and gazed at her, to make sure this was not a dream. Then he reached out to touch her cheek and trailed his hand down her neck and across her breasts.

She nodded. Too moved to speak. His touch, his voice, were everything she'd dreamed about. Everything she'd ever wanted.

"I came to tell you I'm sorry. You were right. I was wrong. I've been doing my research. I've learned a lot I didn't know before. Yes, it's true some women with asthma have a hard time during pregnancy. Some women without asthma have a hard time, too. But that doesn't stop them for getting pregnant and having babies.

"There are all kinds of safeguards like careful fetal

monitoring during delivery. The majority of asthma patients do fine. I can't worry about everything. If you've taught me anything it's to take chances. I'm going to lead a normal life. Better than normal, if I have you." She threw her arms around him and hugged him tightly. Hoping against hope that he hadn't changed his mind.

He held her by the shoulders and looked deep into her eyes and she saw his love burning brightly for her. He took her hand and pressed it against his heart. "Hear that?"

She heard it. She felt it and she knew the answer to the question she'd come here tonight to ask. "Will you marry me, Max?"

He grinned, his smile dazzling in the moonlight. "I'll marry you right here in this garden where we met, my Sleeping Beauty."

"I've changed since then," she said, looking deep into his eyes. "I've learned to swim for one thing. And I've learned to take chances. If you want children, we'll do whatever it takes."

"I've changed, too. I've learned to deal with the past. I've learned that growing up with parents who should have gotten divorced wasn't reason enough to give up on love and marriage. I knew I didn't want to be unhappy like them, or poor like them. But when I got enough money it still wasn't enough. What I needed was love and understanding. I never thought I'd find it until I met you."

She hugged him tightly. Her throat hurt with the

tears she choked back. "I'll never let you down, Max. I'll love you forever."

After a long time when they finally came up for air, Sarah stepped out of Max's arms. "I've got something to show you," she said. Then she pulled her pale gown off over her head and walked to the edge of the pool, her bare body gleaming in the moonlight.

He gasped at the sight of her long legs, her hips and her breasts silhouetted against the night sky.

"Last one in is a rotten egg," she said. With that she dove into the deep end.

"Sarah!" He stood at the edge of the pool, ready to dive in and rescue her. But she came to the surface, smiling and splashing.

He laughed, overcome with relief and joy, then peeled off his clothes and left them in a heap on the ground. He jumped in and joined her in the water.

"You're full of surprises," he said, grinning at her. "My little history buff is now skinny-dipping."

"Only here, only with you," she said.

"What about your hero, Secundino?"

She gave him an impish smile that was one part Sarah and one part nineteenth century shameless flirt.

"Gone forever. You're my hero now. Now and forever. I love you, Max." And she sealed it with a warm wet kiss.

Epilogue

The day was cool and breezy. The guests gathered in the groom's patio where a few dozen chairs were set up. Gardenias floated in the swimming pool, filling the air with a divine fragrance.

A string quartet on the patio began playing and the guests took their places. From the house next door a glowing bride in white satin, her dark hair held back with a pearl crown, came walking on her father's arm down the path and through the gate onto the terrace. Heads turned and there was a collective sigh of admiration.

The simple ceremony took place under a trellis covered with purple morning glories. There were no poems, or odes to the bride or groom. Just the vows that men and women have been taking for hundreds of years. When the bride and groom kissed, the bride's aunt wiped tears of joy from her eyes.

"Well, Mary, I suppose you planned this whole thing," Sarah's mother told her sister.

"Who me?" Mary said innocently but with a twinkle in her eye. "If I've learned one thing in my life it's that you can't plan love. It sneaks up on you when you least expect it." She took the hand of the tall grayhaired man who was standing next to her.

"Ruth, I don't believe you've met Henry," Mary said. "He's a friend from that cruise I was on. Henry's here on vacation. We're going to be taking care of Max's house while they're on their honeymoon."

"Where are they going?" Sarah's mother asked. "I don't think I heard."

"I recommended a cruise," Mary said. "There's nothing as romantic."

"Despite what happened on your cruise?" Sarah's mother asked, aghast.

"Despite everything. No matter what happens, Sarah can handle it. After all, she handled my house, my tree and my neighbor while she was here."

Sarah's boss Trudy congratulated the newlyweds.

"This is a beautiful wedding," Trudy said. "Just like a fairy tale."

Max looked at his bride and squeezed her hand. "I think I know which one you mean."

And just like the prince and Sleeping Beauty, Max and Sarah lived happily ever after.

* * * * *

Be sure to watch for a modern version of Snow White as Carol Grace's **FAIRY-TALE BRIDES** *miniseries continues in Silhouette Romance in March 2006.*

SILHOUETTE *Romance*®

Shannon O'Rourke had made
Alex Mackenzie's withdrawn son
laugh…when even *he* had failed.
For that, he could kiss her.

**Where was mistletoe
when you needed it?**

Meet Me Under
the Mistletoe

by

JULIANNA MORRIS

Silhouette Romance #1796

**On sale
December 2005!**

Only from Silhouette Books!